STOLEN STALLION

Many men had set out to capture a magnificent stallion named Parade, but none had yet triumphed through the hardships to gain the ultimate prize.

Silvertip was a dangerous cowboy who could rip out the heart of a mountain lion with his bare hands and when he hunted Parade he took only a rope and raw courage. But trailing him, guns at their sides, were two killers who wanted the cowboy as badly as they wanted the horse!

Max Brand® is the best known pen name of Frederick Faust, creator of Dr Kildare™, Destry, and many other fictional characters popular with readers and viewers worldwide. Faust wrote for a variety of audiences in many genres. His enormous output totalling approximately thirty million words or the equivalent of 530 ordinary books, covered nearly every field: crime, fantasy, historical romance, espionage, Westerns, science fiction, adventure, animal stories, love, war, and fashionable society, big business and big medicine. Eighty motion pictures have been based on his work along with many radio and television programs. For good measure he also published four volumes of poetry. Perhaps no other author has reached more people in more different ways.

Born in Seattle in 1892, orphaned early, Faust grew up in the rural San Joaquin Valley of California. At Berkeley he became a student rebel and one-man literary movement, contributing prodigiously to all campus publications. Denied a degree because of unconventional conduct, he embarked on a series of adventures culminating in New York City where, after a period of near starvation, he received simultaneous recognition as a serious poet and successful popular-prose writer. Later, he traveled widely, making his home in New York, then in Florence, and finally in Los Angeles.

Once the United States entered the Second World War, Faust abandoned his lucrative writing career and his work as a screenwriter to serve as a war correspondent with the infantry in Italy, despite his fifty-one years and a bad heart. He was killed during a night attack on a hilltop village held by the German army. New books based on magazine serials or unpublished manuscripts continue to appear. Alive and dead he has averaged a new one every four months for seventy-five years. In the U.S. alone nine publishers issue his work, plus many more in foreign countries. Yet, only recently have the full dimensions of this extraordinarily versatile and prolific writer come to be recognized and his stature as a protean literary figure in the 20th Century acknowledged. His popularity continues to grow throughout the world.

STOLEN STALLION

Max Brand®

GUNSMOKE

First published by Hodder & Stoughton

This hardback edition 2004
by BBC Audiobooks Ltd
by arrangement with
Golden West Literary Agency

ISBN 1 4056 8010 5

British Library Cataloguing in Publication Data available.

Printed and bound in Great Britain by
Antony Rowe Ltd., Chippenham, Wiltshire

CONTENTS

5

STOLEN STALLION

CHAPTER I

BRANDY

HE STOOD SIXTEEN THREE, BUT HIS HOOFS PRESSED THE ground like the paws of a cat. Wherever the moonlight fingered him, shoulder or flank, it touched on silk. With head raised, he looked into the wind, and there seemed in him a lightness of spirit, as though he were capable of leaping into the air and striding on it; but the leather crossbars of a halter were fitted over his head and a lead rope trailed down into the hand of Lake, the half-breed. The stallion, that looked as much king of the earth as ever a hawk was king of the sky, was tied fast to a brutal humanity.

Lake turned his savage face. The same moon that lingered on the beauty of the horse etched out the ugliness of the man with a few high lights and skull-like shadows.

"What's he called?" asked Lake.

Harry Richmond was grinning, for he understood the excitement that was making the voice of Lake hard and quick.

"Brandy's his name," said Richmond. "And that's what he's like, ain't he? A regular shot under the belt, eh?"

He moved to another position, so that he could examine the stallion anew with familiar but ever-delighted eyes. Richmond had the lean legs of a rider and a fat lump of a body mounted on them, so that he looked like a blue crane when it stands at the margin of water with its head laid back on its shoulders, readier for sleep than for frogs.

"Looks ain't the hoss," Lake was saying. "But where'd you get this one? You never had nothing on your ranch but mustangs that was rags and bones, and this here is a thoroughbred."

"Yeah," agreed the rancher, "he makes even Mischief look pretty sick, don't he?"

He pointed toward the big mare which stood near by. Mischief seemed nothing, after the stallion, but any good judge who narrowed his eyes could not fail to see her points. She had been caught wild off the range and never more than half tamed; but, like a wild-caught hawk, she seemed able to move without tiring. In every rodeo race where she was entered, the cowpunchers were sure to back her with their money, and she never yet had failed them.

"Maybe he has looks," reiterated Lake, "but looks ain't the hoss. Take and run 'em, and Mischief would likely eat him up."

"That's what we're goin' to see," answered Harry Richmond. "That's why I got you down here, Lake. I'll pay you ten dollars, if you'll run the mare a mile or two against that stallion."

Lake shook his head with a movement so slow that he seemed merely to be looking over each shoulder. "I won't run Mischief for ten, but I'll race her for fifty," he declared.

"For fifty!" exclaimed Richmond. "And me ridin' Brandy? Me givin' you more'n a pound for every dollar of the bet? I ain't such a fool."

"Then it ain't a go," said Lake. "I'll run Mischief yonder to the top of that hill, where the rocks stick out and back here for a finish."

"Two miles, and a lump like me ridin' against a skinny buzzard of a jockey like you?" protested Richmond. But then his eye ran over the silk and the shine of Brandy, and he said through his teeth, "I'll do it!"

He picked up a saddle and bridle, and began to prepare the stallion.

Lake made a cigarette and presently was blowing dissolving wreaths of smoke into the moonshine.

"Look!" he commanded, and waved his hand toward the rattletrap barn near which they were standing, and toward the broken-backed house beyond, and then to the hills and hollows of the ranch, naked as waves of the sea. "Look" said Lake. "You never raised no horse like Brandy on this kind of a place, and you never paid for him out of your pocket. Where'd you get him?"

"I only got half of him," said Richmond, "but, if he can run the way I think, I'll have the other half, too."

"Who owns the other half?" asked Lake.

"You know Charlie Moore?"

"That old cowpuncher of yours? That cockeyed one?"

"That's him. He owns the other half," answered Richmond. "Three or four years back, Charlie Moore was over at the railroad station in Parmalee, and a train pulls in, and on that train there's the racin' stable of Sam Dickery, the big oil man and crook. And they take off a dead mare, a brood mare by the name of Mary Anne, that had had a foal before her time; the foal was carted off, too, not strong enough to stand. It was the get of Single Shot, that foal was, and the stable manager cursed the hair off the head of the veterinary who said he couldn't save the colt. Anyway, they got ready to knock the foal on the head when old Charlie Moore—that never did have no sense— said he'd like to have the colt. Dickery's trainer grinned and said the deal was on, and all it would cost Charlie was the price of diggin' the grave. But Charlie spent a week right there on the spot, and never moved until he got that colt onto its feet; and here it is today—Brandy!"

"Yeah," said Lake, "that's why Brandy has a kind of hand-polished look about him. Every fool in the world has got one good thing in him, I guess, and this is what Charlie Moore's done with his life. But how come that you got a half claim in the horse?"

As he spoke, Lake began to dig softly, with the tips of his fingers, among the India-rubber strands of muscles which overlaid the shoulder of Brandy.

Harry Richmond thrust out his head with a laugh, saying, "Moore's a half-wit, just about. He never has any money. The boys do him out of his month's pay before he ever gets close to a saloon. So when the colt got sick a couple times and needed a vet, I took a chance and paid the bills, and pulled a half interest out of Moore. That was when Brandy was more'n a year old, and I could see that he was goin' to be somethin'. It was like takin' half the teeth out of Moore's head, but he signed up a paper with me. And I'm goin' to get the other half of Brandy, too, if he can make a fool out of Mischief. Ready?"

They sat the saddles side by side, with Mischief already sensing the contest and beginning to dance for it, while Brandy fell to looking once more into the eye of the wind that brought to his nostrils so many tales from the unknown range.

That was why, when the count of ten was finished, Mischief shot off many a length in the lead; Harry Richmond, thinking of his fifty dollars, began to curse, calling Lake back for a "fair start." The words were blown off his lips. There is something in every hot-blooded horse that can sense a race, and Brandy went after Mischief like a hurled spear.

It was soft, sandy going over which Mischief dusted along lightly, while the pounding hoofs of Brandy broke through, flinging up handfuls of sand that puffed out into clouds. They had six furlongs of such going before they struck the steep slope of the hills, and Richmond waited for that ascent to quench the speed of the stallion. Instead, Brandy went up that rise like a bounding mule deer, and collared the mare at the rocks, where they turned.

A cry came suddenly out of the throat of Richmond. He struck the stallion with the flat of his hand. And then he found himself leaning backward, fighting to get into an upright position, for the mount seemed to be leaping out from under the rider. Brandy had twisted his head a little to the side, in the full fury of his effort, as though he were about to turn a corner, and nothing could have been stranger than to see him boring his head so crookedly into the wind. One might have thought that he was looking back for orders from his rider.

That was the end of the race. As Richmond went by, his heart lifted into his throat by the prodigious striding of the stallion, he saw the face of Lake convulsed with malice and disbelief. And when Richmond pulled up at the starting point behind the barn, the mare was thirty lengths behind.

The half-breed had nothing to say. He dismounted, threw the reins, and then stepped back to watch the dropped head, the heaving sides, the sweat that ran in a steady trickle from the belly of Mischief. As for Brandy, he was merely polished black by the run, and seemed on tip-toe for another race.

Still in silence, Lake drew out his wallet to pay the bet.

"Wait a minute," protested Richmond. "Fifty dollars will break you. I'm goin' to give you money, not take it away."

"She lay down and quit!" said Lake fiercely.

"She didn't quit," answered Richmond. "She'll go right on winnin' all kinds of races at the rodeos; but, the way Brandy come wingin' past her, he would 'a' beat pretty near any hoss in the world. He's goin' to get his chance, too. Listen to me, Lake! You got the wool pulled out of your ears and your brain tuned up?"

"What kind of a crooked deal?" asked Lake.

"It ain't crooked," declared Richmond. "You take a poor half-wit like Charlie Moore, what would he do with a stake hoss? He wouldn't know. But you and *me* would know. You hear me, Lake? This here Brandy has gotta go East, and pick up a new name, and he's goin' to meet the best in the land—for the biggest stakes. I can't leave the ranch—there's too much money for me right here in beef —but *you're* free, Lake. You're goin' to take Brandy tomorrow night, and you're goin' to start East with him. You're goin' to clean up, and you and me go half and half!"

The half-breed looked at Richmond and grinned. Then he put back his ugly face so that the moonlight flooded it, and laughed silently.

CHAPTER II

SILVERTIP

THE PLANS WHICH THE RANCHER AND THE HALF-BREED laid by moonlight were perfectly definite and simple. Lake was to come the following night, after Richmond had scraped together some money to cover expenses on the trip to the East. The half-breed was to steal Brandy and make for the railroad, not at the town of Parmalee, close at hand, but far to the north. On the road he could ship Brandy to the East, and inside of three weeks the big horse might be appearing on the tracks. It was a scheme that promised the greater success because the crime in which they shared would force them to a mutual honesty in their own dealings.

But next morning a message came. A messenger rode out from Parmalee with a brief letter from Lake to Richmond. The rancher read:

Dear Richmond: The game is off for a while. I've had a glimpse of Charlie Moore in town, and he was drinking with Silvertip. Why didn't you tell me that Silver was Moore's friend? Silvertip would as soon take a shot at me as at a mountain grouse. I'm laying low till he leaves this part of the range.

Lake.

The name of Silvertip was unknown to Harry Richmond. He burned the letter and went in search of information. Since the punchers were out on the range, he went into the kitchen with his questions; the cook stopped peeling potatoes while he answered.

"I never seen Silvertip no more'n I ever seen wire gold," said the "doctor," as the cook was sometimes called, "But I've heard gents talk about him, here and there. He gets his name from a coupla streaks of gray hair over his temples, but he ain't old. He ain't thirty. He's ripped the top ground off a fortune twenty times, but he never stops long enough to dig out the pay dirt, because he's always in a hurry. Trouble is what he hunts for breakfast, kills it for lunch, and eats it for supper."

"What kind of trouble?" asked Harry Richmond, gnawing his fleshy lip.

"Any kind," said the cook. "A hoss that pitches right smart is his kind of a hoss; a forest on fire is his kind of a forest; a gold-rush town is his kind of a town; and a two-gun fightin' man is his kind of a man."

"They ought to outlaw that kind of a hound," said the rancher angrily.

"No," said the cook. "He ain't any trouble to a sheriff; he's more of a help. Coupla years back, down in Brown's Creek, when the gold rush come and half the yeggs in the country flocked in, the regular, honest miners, they got together and they sent an invitation to Silvertip to go and settle down with them for a while. And he went. And that was a loud town, Richmond. That was a town that you could hear all the way across the mountains. But after Silvertip was there a week, he soothed it down such a lot that you couldn't hear a whisper out of it."

"He killed the bad actors, you mean?" asked Richmond.

"I dunno that he killed any. I hear that mostly he can shoot so straight that he don't have to kill; and when he comes in one door, the yeggs go out the other."

Richmond went off to digest this news, agreeing in his

mind to despise Lake less than when the half-breed's letter had arrived. The rattling wheels of an approaching buckboard brought him out of the house, and he saw Charlie Moore drive up with a big stranger on the seat beside him. The stranger's mount, a big bay gelding with chasings of silver aflash on it, jogged behind the rig, which was loaded with the supplies which Moore had been sent to buy the evening before. It was the simplest way of getting him off the place while Lake arrived to test the stallion.

Charlie Moore drew up near the kitchen door and climbed to the ground; his big companion glided down with one step, as though from a saddle.

"Meet Silvertip, Mr. Richmond—Harry Richmond," said Charlie Moore. He smiled with pride to be presenting such a famous man.

Harry Richmond stepped forward with a grunt and a grin, but the manners of Silvertip were rather more Latin than American. He took off his hat and bowed a little to the rancher, as he shook hands. Richmond saw, above the temples, the spots of gray, and an odd chill passed through him.

It was a brown face that he looked into, and the expression was full of such gentle peace as the rancher had never seen before. It was the look of one who daydreams, with the faintest of smiles continually about the lips. Never was a face more handsome, more honest, more open; and yet the chill was still working in the spinal marrow of Richmond. Brandy, and all the fortune that could be made out of the great horse, was as good as his own, until the arrival of Silvertip. Now he felt that good fortune had withdrawn many miles from him.

They began to unload the buckboard together. The flour sacks, the sides of bacon, the hams, were easily handled. But when it came to the big two-hundred-pound sacks of potatoes, which Richmond and old Charlie Moore struggled with together, Silver picked them up by the ears and carried the burden easily into the storeroom.

"He's strong," said the rancher.

"Aye," said Charlie Moore, wagging his head in admiration. "He's mighty strong. He's too strong. A gent like that is too strong to work."

There was a meaning behind this remark which Harry

Richmond appreciated to the full, and he looked suddenly and sharply at Moore, as though wondering how far that simple-minded fellow could have looked into a man like Silvertip. But there was nothing to be seen in the face of Moore other than his usual expression, which was that of a child half dreaming over the world and half hurt by it.

Moore looked much younger than his fifty-five years, except for the pain which had worked in the lines about the mouth and in the center of the forehead. But his hair was still dark, and his eyes were still bright. His clothes were those of any hard-working cowpuncher, except that his boots were common cowhide—and where does one find a self-respecting cowpuncher, who is without meticulous pride in his footwear? But there was no pride in Charlie Moore. He had gone all his life quite content if he could avoid trouble and understand the need of the moment, and the commands which were given to him. He was not, like Silvertip, "a gent too strong to work!"

To be sure, Silvertip was walking by again with the weight of another sack trundled comfortably in his arms. As he passed, Harry Richmond looked askance and saw the great spring of muscles that arched from shoulder to shoulder, the corseting of might which gripped him about the loins and swelled his torso above hips as lean as those of a desert wolf that can run all day and fight all night. That was what Silvertip seemed to Harry Richmond—a machine too flawless to be used on the mere mechanics of ranch work.

"Silvertip, he's an old friend of mine," said Charlie Moore, dusting the white of flour from his coat sleeves, as the unloading of the wagon was finished. "I guess," he added, with a sudden wistfulness, "that Silver's about the best friend that I got!" He blundered on: "Which ain't meanin' that Silvertip takes me very serious. Nobody does. But I guess he means more to me than anybody else."

Harry Richmond, watching very closely, saw the smile struck from the mouth of Silvertip; but at the same instant the hand of Silver went out and rested for a moment on the shoulder of Moore. The latter seemed to accept that touch as an assurance of all that he could have wished. He brightened; with an air of surprised happiness, he

16

looked up at Silvertip, who avoided that glance by saying to Richmond:

"Charlie tells me that you and he have a great horse out here."

"Pretty fair—pretty fair," answered Richmond. With an air of thought, he pursed his mouth until the tip of his nose was raised, and his fat face was sculptured into a new and amazing design. "Soft—but I'll tell you what he's got, that Brandy. He's got pretty good lines. That's why I could use him with some mustang mares and get me some saddle stock. I'll tell you what, Charlie—I'll buy out your half in Brandy. He ain't much. He's too heavy and soggy, kind of, in the quarters. But I'm tired of this partnership business, and I'll buy him off you. I'll give you a good price for your share, too. Whatcha want, Charlie? Speak up and name your price."

"Sell my half of Brandy?" asked Moore, staring like a round-eyed child. He laughed a little, but the pain remained in his blue eyes. "I could easier sell half of myself," he concluded.

"Now, don't you be a fool," said Richmond. He stepped closer, so that the superiority of his bulk might impress itself on the eye of Moore as the weight of his words impressed itself on the simple mind of the puncher. He laid the tip of a forefinger like a dagger at the breast of his ranch hand. "Who knows more about business, you or me?" he demanded.

"Why, you do, Harry," answered Moore, instantly abashed. "Sure, you know a lot more than I do."

"Then don't be a fool," went on Richmond. "I'm goin' to pay you your own price. I'll pay you up to six months' wages. Not that half of Brandy is worth that much, but just because I wanta get rid of the argument. I hate argument. You know that. I'm goin' to give you a chance to pick up a price of good money, Charlie; I'm goin' to show you that I'm your friend."

For it seemed to Richmond that this was the time to strike, and strike hard, for the prize, before Silvertip laid his wise eye on the stallion and saw Brandy's real value. And Charlie Moore, amazed and baffled and somewhat agape as he listened to the impressive words of Richmond, rolled his eyes from side to side.

The quiet voice of Silvertip broke in: "No man will

sell the blood out of his body, Richmond, and that's what Brandy is to Charlie. Let's put up the team and have a look at the horse."

Charlie Moore heaved a sigh of relief; Richmond bit his lip. But by those few words the matter seemed to be settled beyond appeal. If Richmond wanted the stallion, he would, in fact, have to steal him. And he cursed Silvertip with a silent fervor.

They put up the mustangs, ran the buckboard into the wagon shed, and went to the big corral behind the barn, where Brandy was grazing. He could have had his name for his color; he was a golden fire, red-stained and sun-burnished. At the whistle of Moore, he picked up his head from his grazing and turned suddenly about. Black silk covered his legs to the knees and the hocks; black velvet covered his muzzle; and between the eyes there was a white wedge, like the hallmark of the Master Maker.

"Kind of soft all over," said Richmond. "Kind of heavy and soggy in the quarters, ain't he? But sort of good-lookin'; picture-book hoss, that kids would be crazy about. That's all."

But a faint cry had come out of the throat of Silvertip. He was through the bars of the fence and stepping across toward the stallion with hand extended. Charlie Moore made so free as to grasp the arm of Richmond with a frantic hand.

"Look! Look!" said Moore. "It's even the kind of a horse for Silvertip. It's the kind of a horse he wants, and he's never wanted a horse before."

"How come?" asked Richmond angrily. "How come you say he never has wanted a hoss before?"

"Look at what I mean," muttered Charlie, keeping enchanted eyes upon the picture of Silvertip approaching the stallion. "What I mean is that Silver, he never finds nothin' that he really wants. That's why he never stops still. There ain't no girl pretty enough to stop him for a week. There ain't no house right enough to be his home. There ain't no mine rich enough to keep him diggin'. There ain't no man big enough to be his friend. There ain't no horse fine enough for him to make a partner of it. No horse before Brandy, maybe! But look at Silver now! Look at the way he's steppin' around him. Look at him measurin' and measurin' and admirin'—"

18

"There ain't much in this world that Silvertip's interested in except a fight—is that it?" asked the rancher.

"That and danger," said Charlie Moore absently. "There's danger been put into the world, and there's men been put to love it, I guess. Why, he ain't even satisfied with Brandy—not even with him! Look at Silver shakin' his head a little and shruggin' his shoulders. And here he comes back to us. Hey, Silver!" he called. "Don't you make up your mind till you've tried him. Don't you damn Brandy till you've tried him, will you?"

"Of course I'll try him," said Silvertip. "And he's a grand horse. No wonder you're proud of him, Charlie. He's the finest for his weight that I ever saw. Just for a minute I almost thought—well, no matter about that."

He broke off with a sigh, and his eyes went regretfully back toward the stallion.

"You thought what? You almost thought what?" asked Moore eagerly. "You thought almost that he would be the horse for *you,* Silver? Ain't that what you almost thought? Try him, Silver, and maybe he *is* the horse for you. If he is, you can have him. I'll give him up. It'd be better to me than ownin' him to think of you and him out together, like a coupla kings, like a coupla hawks flyin' over the mountains. You try him, and if he *is* your horse, you can have him. It'd do me good, day and night, to think of you two together."

The hand of Silvertip rested again on the shoulder of Moore, and his glance went deeply into the face of the cowpuncher, for an instant.

"You're a kind fellow, Charlie," he said. "One of these days I'm afraid that you'll give away your heart and soul —because you'll find somebody else who could use 'em!"

"About givin' Brandy away," said Richmond angrily, "that's a kind of a joke, ain't it? Or maybe I don't own half of him."

The quiet eyes, the quiet voice of Silvertip turned toward Richmond, as he answered: "I can buy your half of the horse, Richmond. A half interest is only worth six months of Charlie's pay, isn't it? That's the top price that I heard you put on him."

A hot retort swelled the throat of Richmond, and died in it. For suddenly he knew, not by reputation only, that this man was dangerous.

"I'll get a saddle on Brandy. You try him," Moore was saying.

So saddle and bridle were put on the stallion, Brandy opening his mouth for the bit as though it were a thing to eat. Then Silvertip mounted, sliding into the saddle as though he were stepping onto the back of a pony. This man made all things seem small and easy.

Afterward, he rode Brandy out of the corral, down into the hollow, jumped the dry ditch there, and brought the horse swinging back. Charlie Moore was white with eagerness and questions when the big man dismounted. A gentle consideration appeared in the face of Silver as he regarded Moore.

"It's a glorious horse; it's a wonderful horse, Charlie," said Silvertip. "It's as fine a horse as I ever had under me —or finer."

"But not for you?" asked Moore huskily, working at the cinch knot with fingers that seemed suddenly too weak to handle the strap.

"You know how people are," answered Silvertip, more gently than ever. "It's only when a thing fits into the mind like a word into a line—it's only then that a fellow will give up his blood to get what he wants. That's the only time. But if Brandy were just a hair different, I'd give my soul for him; I'd trail him down on foot to get him!"

His head and his voice had lifted. He seemed to be looking into the future. And, in fact, he was making a phophecy, though not exactly of the sort he had in mind.

"Well," said Charlie Moore sadly, "he fits into my ideas, all right. He suits me well enough. Poor old Brandy! Poor old boy!"

He put the stallion back into the corral, while Richmond, with a breath of relief, turned on his heel and went back to the house, satisfied that Silvertip would not try to buy the stallion. His satisfaction would have been much less if he could have overheard Silvertip at the corral fence saying to Moore:

"Mind you, Charlie, Richmond wants that stallion, and he's going to have him unless you look sharp. I won't be around here very long, but, while I'm near, I'm going to help you watch. The hand is faster than the eye, Charlie, and this fellow Richmond has the look of a thief about him."

CHAPTER III

LAKE TAKES THE CHANCE

RICHMOND WENT INTO THE TOWN OF PARMALEE THAT same day, and found the half-breed, Lake, hidden out in a little Mexican tavern at the edge of the village. In the dimness of the back room they talked together; their eyes and their whisky glasses glistened; their voices were so soft that they melted into the shadows of the place.

"I've seen Silvertip," said Richmond, squeezing his fat fingers around his glass. "And he's plenty to look at."

"He'd go in the dark into a hole in the ground and rip the heart out of a mountain lion with his bare hands," said Lake. "That's all he would do. I've seen quarters throwed up into the air, spinning, and I've seen him shoot 'em, with never a miss."

"Can he do that?" said Richmond.

"He can," said Lake.

After that, in a silence, they drank their whiskies. Something more than the rankness of the drink made Richmond shudder. Then he went on:

"Silvertip don't like me. He looked me in the face like a buzzard at a dyin' steer. Seemed like he wanted to be at me. He's workin' on that fool of a Charlie Moore, too, tellin' him how much money Brandy is worth. And the thing to do is to act right now. Lake, you're goin' to sneak over to the place this evenin' and take Brandy, and skin out with him. Understand?"

"I hear you talk," said Lake. He laughed with a light hissing sound. "I hear you talk like a fool!" he added. "While Silvertip's around? No, no, brother! I'm goin' to lay low like a chipmunk in a hole till that hombre is out of sight!"

"What you so scared of him for? What you ever done to him?" demanded Richmond, angry with impatience.

"I never done nothin' to him," said Lake. "I ain't such a fool to try my hand on Silvertip. But one night I was havin' a time for myself in a saloon—and it don't matter where—and he come and dropped in and seen what I was doin'. I got away by divin' through a window and takin' the glass with me."

He raised his hand to his face and delicately traced the course of a scar with the tip of his finger.

"Listen to me," said Richmond. "You're broke. You're flat. I'm goin' to stake you to five hundred bucks. Understand? Five hundred iron men!"

He pulled out his wallet.

"Feed your money to swine," said Lake. "I don't want it. It's only goin' to choke me—while Silver's around."

But Richmond began to lay out the greenbacks, one after the other. They made a soft and secret whispering.

"Five—hundred—dollars!" said Richmond, pushing the stack across the table. "That'll see you all the way East with Brandy. And after that—the big money for the both of us!"

"Take it away. I don't want it. I won't risk my neck. Not while Silvertip's around!" groaned Lake.

Suddenly he clutched the pile of soft paper and crunched it into the palm of his hand.

"It's cuttin' my throat," he said through his teeth, "but I'll take the chance. While you're sleepin' soft, I'll take the chance. You'll be dead asleep, and I'll be dead on the ground. That's the way it works. The gent that has the money always gets the best deal. I hope you rot!"

"Do you?" said Richmond, with a yawn. "Have another drink."

"I don't want no more. I've had too much already. I don't want no liquor on board of me while I'm within fifty miles of Silvertip. Go on and get out and leave me alone. I gotta do some plannin'."

The planning of the half-breed kept him motionless in that dark little room through most of the remainder of the day. He sketched in his mind every detail of Richmond's ranch—the house, the barn, the corral, the devious ways among the naked hills. If there had only been a growth of trees, how much more securely he might have approached the thought of the stealing of Brandy!

It was almost dusk when he left Parmalee and rode toward the Richmond ranch; it was in the thick of the night when he saw the light from a bedroom window throwing frail yellow spars of brilliance against his eyes.

He came up like an Indian, making a complete circle about the place, then drifting in at angles until he had reached the corral behind the barn. The moon would be up before long; yes, the pale hand of it was already climbing in the east.

The thought of the brightness that would soon flood the earth made the heart of Lake twist and shrink in his breast. But now, out of the ground shadows, arose the form of a great horse, and he knew that it was Brandy, standing up to sniff at a stranger in the night.

Lake remembered suddenly how the stallion had breezed past him, making Mischief seem to stand still. There was money—there was a fortune in that horse. Mischief was no thoroughbred, but she could last like patience; and yet she had been run off her feet and worn weak by the stallion. What would Brandy do, then, with a perfect track under his hoofs, and a mere feather of a jockey in the saddle?

Across the eye of the half-breed rolled a picture of turreted stands, bright with flags, white with massed faces. He felt along his nerves the vibrancy of ten thousand voices cheering; he saw the field of horses sweeping toward the finish; and then a chestnut stockinged in black silk sweep out from the throng to finish by himself. Brandy! The cheering—the curious and envious gentry— the presentation of the silver cup—the stake money—the flattery from the rich and the great!

He—half-breed Lake—had always known that he could make as good a gentleman as another, when occasion offered. It was merely a matter of money, clothes, and a certain coldly distant manner. But the money was the chief thing—easy money that would take wings again easily.

He slid from the saddle, threw the reins of his mare, and, taking his coiled lariat from the pommel of the saddle, he advanced to the corral and slid between the bars of it. Something seemed to strike at his head, like a hand of darkness. It was merely the flight of an owl, slanting close to the ground. But, with guard still raised, his body still crouching, Lake turned his snarling face and stared for a long time after that night hunter.

He recovered after a moment. Every instant he wasted was a chance for life and success thrown away—for Silvertip might be somewhere near. He might be watching at this moment, smiling his faint smile at the figure of the horse thief caught behind the black bars of the corral fence.

For one thing Lake was profoundly thankful—that the stallion had been handled to the point of absolute docility; for now, as Brandy stood at the farther side of the corral with raised head and shadowy arching tail, he looked capable of bounding in three strides to the distant rising moon. Lake shook out the noose of his rawhide rope and swung it in a widening circle. Carelessly he threw the lariat, still from the corners of his eyes hunting for an enemy that might rise out of the ground. But, even if he had been totally alert, he might have missed, for Brandy leaped sidewise and sprang swiftly across the corral.

The reata, cutting the empty air, struck the ground with a rippling fall, and a slight tremor ran up the hand and arm of Lake. For suppose that the stallion fought? Suppose that the great horse made a sound of trampling and snorting? Suppose that the noise reached the house?

Lake gathered up the frail and snaky shadow of the rope. Hastily he advanced toward the stallion in the corner. Brandy leaped aside, the starlight glancing dimly in the polish of his flanks.

"Now, you high-headed fool!" muttered Lake, and started to whirl his rope as he stepped in for the throw.

That cast was not made. Instead, Lake dodged for his life, as an avalanche of horseflesh hurled suddenly at him, with a glint of eyes and yawning teeth, and a flag of mane blown above.

Right across the corral and around it galloped the stallion, with every stride making the enclosure seem smaller and smaller; and as Brandy ran, he flung his head up and sent through the night a neigh that rang like the blast of a thousand copper horns in the ears of Lake. The blood rushed upward through his brain. He seemed like a child gathering a string into his hand—a foolish child attempting to snare a monster. That challenging call from the stallion would be sure to rouse all the punchers in the house. Most of all, it might reach the ears of that consummate man-slayer, Silvertip!

Yet the half-breed did not run for his life. He shuddered, his very heart quaked in him, but all the Indian of his soul had now rallied to that game of horse stealing. He ran forward, keen-eyed, sure of hand, and snared Brandy with the swift, underarm fling of the rope.

Against the taut lariat the stallion would not pull; Lake ran up the line, hand over hand. Near by, he heard a door slam. It seemed right in his ear, yet he knew that it must have come from the house. A voice called; other voices answered; and, above all, came the beat of hoofs.

Aye, and there in the east, white as frost, brilliant, the eye of the rising moon glanced at him. There was no time to flee now. There was not even time to run to Mischief and be off on her. The danger that approached was a wave whose head already curled above him.

Lake caught the mane of the horse with his left hand, jerked the reata into a noose over Brandy's head, and leaped onto his back. Under Lake, the silk and steel of Brandy flinched, and off to the side, rushing at full speed, was a big rider on a big horse, the brim of the man's sombrero blown flat up by the wind of the gallop. By the width of those shoulders, by something dauntless in that bearing, Lake knew that Silvertip was at him, and with the steel rowels of his spurs, Lake gripped the tender body of the horse.

Brandy groaned, but with his groan he started; he was running away from the pain that burned into his flanks; he was running from a new fear of humankind who never before had harmed him. It was that fear which lifted him at the lofty bars of the corral fence. He skimmed it with his elbows, with his belly. His heels struck so hard his head tipped down.

A yell of fear exploded upward in the throat of Lake. It died as it reached his teeth, for Brandy landed on sure feet and fled straight forward. Mischief, by the startled upfling of her head, tossed the reins across her back and rushed in pursuit.

Lake glanced back. All of this had happened, yet only half of the shining face of the moon was showing above the eastern horizon. Yet that mighty lantern would soon be high, striking him with its rays, showing him to the big rider on the big horse that strode behind. But let him ride with all his cunning, let him be ten times Silvertip, if only Lake could keep on the back of Brandy for another five minutes, he would be out of pistol shot. The wind of the gallop burned his eyes, and still that speed increased.

A shout struck his ears; a bullet pierced the air beside him; the sound of the explosion shook him as though by a strong hand. The half-breed flattened himself along the back of Brandy and clutched the flanks of the stallion anew with his spurs. Right through the velvet of the hide, into the rubbery sheathing of muscles, drove the rowels. Brandy did what he never had done before; he bucked high in the air and landed on stiffened legs.

They were flying down hill at the time. The sharpness of the slope snapped the whip for Brandy and shot Lake off of that smooth bare back. He rolled skidding across the sand. As he got to his knees, he saw Silvertip coming like a giant of wrath, with a revolver poised in his hand. The half-breed screamed. He fell flat on his face, yelling for mercy. Hoofbeats fell near him. Sand squirted into his eyes. But there was no thunderclap of an exploding gun at his ears.

He half rose. Up the farther slope raced Brandy, the snake-like shadow of the lariat flying above him, Mischief laboring in vain pursuit. And yet farther behind them was Silvertip, losing ground at every stride.

The whole body of the moon had risen in the east. Lake turned from that accusing light and threw out his hands before him like a child fleeing from a nightmare. That was how he raced to find shelter, dodging as he ran.

CHAPTER IV

THE VICTOR

FOR THREE MILES SILVERTIP RACED BEHIND THE fugitives. Then he gave it up and settled down to a steady, cautious hunt. The stallion, he was sure, he could have snared at any time, but Mischief made the trouble. Wild-caught, she seemed to have reverted to the wild again. It was she who stood on constant watch; it was she who herded Brandy away at every near approach of the hunter.

On the first night she stepped on a trailing rein and dragged the bridle from her head; on the next day she broke the saddle by rolling, then rose in a frenzy and bucked it off. No sign of man was on her, now, except the brand on her hip.

It was no blind flight. She had a direction in her mind, as surely as a migrating bird. North and west, north and west, she led the way into a region of naked mountains; of great valleys that seemed to have been carved out by the wind, since there were no rivers to flow through them; of plains where the grass grew not at all, or only in scattered tufts. Only the eye of an artist could wander with pleasure among the colored mesas, or from the white of the sands to the blue of the distances. A horse had to rove for miles in order to pick up a meager bellyful, then lope twenty miles in the evening to find water—sucking it out of a muddy hole. But there was one advantage that made the region a paradise for wild horses; if it was a bitter country, burned bone-dry in summer, frozen by terrible winds in the winter, it was all the more free from man. Here and there a prospector voyaged like a snail, sighting his course between the ears of his burro; but no farmer, no cattleman, not even a sheep-herder, would enter this range willingly. And the wild horses knew with a sure instinct that it was better to go half starved in a land free from the tyrant, man, than to fatten for a little while on green pastures in constant danger of rope and gun.

It was on the third day of the hunt that Silvertip, from the brow of a low-running ridge, saw the mare go down the further valley with Brandy at her side, while a dust cloud rose in the distance and rolled against the wind toward them.

They halted. The dust cloud dissolved into a band of twenty loping horses. Brandy stood his ground uneasily, occasionally turning his head to look at the mare. And, meantime, from the rear of the herd, the king of it came sweeping. He was a buckskin with silver mane and tail. He looked like a patch of bright gold in the distance, with a pair of silver flags to blow over him.

The watcher pulled his Winchester out of its saddle holster, and took aim. But right into the circle which his sights covered the buckskin galloped, so that Silvertip dared not fire. At such a distance, his bullet might as well strike one of the swerving, plunging fighters as the other. He lowered the gun and sat, grinning with agony, waiting for the inevitable. He did not even try to rush his horse forward and so interrupt the combat, so certain he was that the wild stallion would kill the tame one out of hand.

He had seen the leaders of the ranging bands struggle together long before this. Like tigers they fought, each toughened by a hundred battles, kicking, striking, above all striving for a throat hold which would end the strife with one wrench and a tear. How could Brandy, no matter what his superiority in size, stand for an instant against such a trained combatant?

In came the buckskin like a dancer, swerving to this side, then to that, before he closed, lunging to take hold on the throat. Missing that vital point, nevertheless the weight of his charge behind his shoulder was enough to knock Brandy head over heels.

That would be the end. Silvertip closed his eyes, unwilling to see that wild beast of the range leap on the fallen body of the thoroughbred and knock it to pieces. But when he looked again, Brandy was up, the buckskin leaping far off to avoid the drive of the reaching hind legs.

Brandy whirled to meet the next charge, and Silver could have sworn that the buckskin got the throat hold, only to have it broken as the taller stallion reared. Upon the crest of the buckskin fell a shower of strokes from the armed forefeet of Brandy. The wild horse fell to his knees, swayed staggering to his feet, and fled before the victorious charge of the stranger.

Silvertip, agape, laughed with joy. He saw the buckskin halt, far off, while Brandy kept his place with a lofty front, as though disdaining to pursue a beaten enemy. Mischief came to his side and touched noses with him. The mares and the younger colts of the wild herd advanced by degrees. Curiosity drew them inexorably. Sometimes the scent of man or the sight of the rawhide lariat about the neck of Brandy sent them scampering, but again and again they returned, until a thick cluster had formed about their new companion.

Mischief broke up the cluster. She advanced up the valley at a steady lope. Brandy followed her; he ranged ahead and the whole herd flooded after; and far to the rear, with fallen crest, came the deposed buckskin leader at a slow trot.

Silvertip watched them for a long time through the clear mountain air. Not a sound came to him. The dust cloud thickened. Finally, it was rolling without a sign of the life that thronged beneath it, and Silvertip shook his head.

If, as he had told Charlie, the chestnut stallion had been a trifle different, he would have given years of his life to secure the horse. But there was something lacking. In Brandy was not the spark that could set the soul of the wanderer on fire, and already he had given three priceless days to this pursuit. He looked toward the horizon. Somewhere beyond it, the great adventure was still waiting for him. Reluctantly he turned his horse, and jogged steadily toward the south.

CHAPTER V

THE HORSE HUNT

THE LETTER WHICH CAME FOR CHARLIE MOORE TO THE Richmond ranch was very crisp and brief. But Charlie read it over and over, sitting in the twilight on the steps of the house while the other cowpunchers sat around their poker game inside. It was near the end of the month, and they were gambling, therefore, in futurities.

Harry Richmond, noisily stalking through the room, more like a fat-bodied, long-legged crane than ever, plucked the paper out of the limp fingers of Moore and read:

Dear Charlie: I was ten seconds too late, the night that Brandy was stolen. That Indian half-breed, Lake, is the rat that ran off with him. Brandy bucked him off before I had a chance to shoot him off. I should have killed the brute while he rolled on the ground, but it's hard to finish off a man who's yelling for mercy. So I went on and trailed Brandy and the mare, Mischief, up into the Sierra Blanca desert. I saw them meet up with a herd of twenty head of wild mustangs and I saw Brandy lick the buckskin leader and take charge of the lot. You know it's no easy business to run down a wild herd. At least, it's about as hard for one man to do the trick as it is to run a flock of wild geese out of the sky. I gave up the job. I have something to do a good bit south of here, and I'm headed in that direction. In the meantime, I thought I'd let you know where Brandy is wandering. Sorry that I couldn't bring him back on a rope to you. But you'll probably need a big outfit of men and horses to run that herd down and get the stallion back. Best of luck to you. I'll try to see you on my way north. If you run across Lake, let him know that his trail means a good deal to me, and that I hope to spend some time on it before long. The yellow hound!

Yours,

Silvertip

When Harry Richmond had finished reading this document, he balled it in his hand and hurled it into the outer darkness.

"Sierra Blanca!" he groaned.

Charlie Moore nodded his head, and swallowed slowly. At last he said, "He's gone. I'll never see Brandy again!"

"If you took care of what you own," shouted Richmond, "if you didn't let sneakin' half-breeds steal everything you've got, you might amount to somethin', some day. Now Brandy's gone. You've let him get away—and half of him was mine."

"Aye," said Charlie Moore, "half of him was yours. And half was mine. And he's gone. I'd give up my half for the chance of seein' him inside the corral once more, liftin' his head when I talk to him, comin' when I whistle. But he's gone into the Sierra Blanca, and nobody'll lay eyes on him again."

A thought struck into the mind of Richmond, deeper than the sound of a bell.

"You'd give him up—your half of him?" asked Richmond.

"I'd give him up," said Charlie Moore, "but that won't bring him back here. I might as well just give up a wish as to give up a horse that's runnin' wild in the Sierra Blanca."

"I dunno," said Harry Richmond. The greatness of his

30

desire and his hope raised a storm in his breast. His eyes burned. "Suppose that you and me and a bunch of others, with some fast horses, went up there and campaigned for Brandy. Suppose that we caught him—you'd give up your half?"

"Sure," said Charlie Moore, "but there ain't any hope."

"There's hope enough to make me try," said the rancher. "Besides," he added, "it would be the same as though he was part yours, anyway. You'd have the handlin' of him!"

It was Mischief that smelled the scent of men and iron and gunpowder before any of the herd. She had been as wild as any of them during half her life, and the other half had familiarized her more profoundly with man and his ways. So her hair-trigger senses found the danger while it was still far off. Her neigh gathered the herd into swift flight that she led, while Brandy ranged at the rear, swinging back and forth, nipping at the old mares, at the ancient, blundering stallions, at the clumsy colts that made up the rear guard. So the herd was partly led and partly swept out of the dangerous narrowness of a valley, and as it ran, the wild horses saw riders streaming down the slope on their left.

On out of the ravine, exploding like a shell in the midst of rolling dust, the herd poured into the more open desert. Behind it the pursuit sagged down, and failed.

But that was only the beginning. For ten days the pursuit continued. Mysteriously, horsemen appeared at the water holes toward which the band headed. Deprived of water and with little time to graze, on account of constant alarms, the whole band lost flesh and strength and spirits—all except Mischief and the new leader. Her iron-hard constitution saved her, and in Brandy there was an unfailing fountain of strength; the greatness of his soul seemed able to supply the needs of his body. Even so, he was drawn fine indeed on that day when the herd had been led into a pleasant valley by Mischief, so that the older and the younger animals could find easier grazing. Here the grass grew almost thick, and two springs threw out rills which joined in a delightful stream before the thirst of the ground sucked up the running water. It was high time that the band should find rest and food; the

31

older animals were beginning to stumble and the knees of the younger colts were continually a-tremble.

They had grazed for perhaps three hours, undisturbed, when the accurate nose of Mischief detected trouble in the offing; her neigh was a clarion that gathered the herd suddenly around her. Brandy joined her on the slight hummock from which she was sweeping the landscape.

"There's no danger," said Brandy, as he touched his nose to hers. "I haven't your eyes, but there's no danger. No horse and rider could manage to sneak up on us, here. Common sense will teach you that."

"Trust a mare's instinct rather than a stallion's common sense," said Mischief, flaring out her nostrils, and stamping suspiciously. "I found the scent of man in the air, and that means trouble."

"A man on horseback—yes," said Brandy.

"Horseback or afoot, it doesn't matter a great deal," said Mischief. "The smell puts the taste of iron back in my mouth, and I feel the rope burn again, and the halter flaps once more on my head. Don't try to tell me, because I know."

"You're afraid," said Brandy.

"I'd rather be afraid ten times than to be caught once," said Mischief. "There!"

As she snorted, Brandy saw a man on foot step out of a patch of brush hardly a hundred yards away. The stallion flinched in turn; the entire herd swerved to flee with Mischief, for the others had learned to defer to her cleverness, her constant watchfulness. More than once the real leader of a herd has been a mare; Mischief was filling that role now.

"Come on!" she called to Brandy.

But he remained where he was. He had lifted his magnificent head, and was studying the slowly advancing figure. A faint wind came from the man to his nostrils.

"There's no scent of a gun," said Brandy. "There's no smell of iron, you know. And there's no rope about him. Why should you be afraid, Mischief?"

"As long as a man has one hand, he's dangerous," said the mare. "Are you coming, Brandy?"

"I'll come presently," said Brandy. "Get the herd down the valley a little. Something makes me want to look at this man a little more closely. I think I know him."

32

Mischief instantly fled a furlong farther down the valley, the other horses packed closely around her. There she paused, and sent her call after her mate. But Brandy was standing his ground. Once or twice he flinched, when Mischief whinnied for him. Yet still he lingered in undecision, for there was something very familiar about that form which came toward him, with hand extended. And now he could hear the voice that passed with a singular magic through all the nerves of his body, soothing him.

It was Charlie Moore, who had come down to try his single hand, where all of the others had failed; the starved, hollow-eyed men of the hunt, the staggering horses, remained high up among the hills, while Moore went down by himself to see what his luck might be.

"Run while you can!" called Mischief, from the distance. "The snake can hold the bird with its eye—and some men can hold a horse, when they come near enough. Run, Brandy!"

Brandy whirled about, tossing his head and then his heels. He slashed his tail right and left, brilliant in the sunshine, before he paused once more. But the half circle in which he ran, had not taken him farther from the approaching figure.

The voice went on. It spoke in sounds which were mostly meaningless, but others were as familiar to Brandy as the speech of his own kind. And, above all, there was the name repeated over and over:

"Brandy! Stand fast, Brandy! Brandy, good boy!"

The stallion let Charlie Moore come straight up to him. When the hand of the man was a yard from his nose, Brandy stretched out his head, sniffed at it, and then bolted at full speed.

Down the valley before him he saw the rest of the herd flying, he heard the rejoiced whinnying of Mischief, and turning in a great circle, Brandy came back almost to the spot where he had confronted Moore before.

His senses were so alert that he could see everything; two buzzards that circled, near and far, in the thin blue of the sky; the thick shadow that dropped along the side of the mesa; the smoke of greasewood that straggled across a nearby hollow; the mist of dust that hung in the air after the passing of the herd. But, most of all, he was aware of the man, the voice, the outstretched hand, the eyes.

What had Mischief said about the eyes of man? These were filled with understanding and gentleness as well. Above all, there was the voice that kept running through his being like a river, and always pouring contented music about his heart.

Far off, Mischief was calling on the highest note of fear and warning.

Brandy shuddered with apprehension, but suddenly he stretched his head to the hand of Moore, saw that hand go past it and grasp the tattered end of the lariat which still hung from his neck. A sobbing noise came out of the throat of Charlie Moore, a sound which Brandy had never heard before. He turned his head to nuzzle the man's shoulder. Still the grip of Moore was on the end of the rope. Freedom had passed from Brandy at that instant, but he hardly cared, for the caressing words dulled him like an opiate. And what was all the wild freedom in this world, compared with the touch of that hand, as it ran down along his neck, and the penetrating, reassuring music of that voice, filled with promises that green pastures and bright waters alone could not fulfill?

CHAPTER VI

PARADE

THAT WAS HOW BRANDY WENT BACK TO THE HANDS OF men, while Mischief led the herd far off into the intricacies of the Sierra Blanca. Sometimes, in the dawn and in the dusk of the day, she ran out from the rest, or lingered behind them, waiting and watching; but she knew, nevertheless, that there was no real hope, and that what men have taken they will not surrender again. They hold what they put their hands on, and no power except that of other men can remove the prize.

There were more things for Mischief to give heed to than the disappearance of Brandy, however. The buckskin leader was still with the herd, but after his downfall his authority could never again be complete.

There was now no voice that the band followed readily except the whinny of the mare. Her tossing mane was what they looked toward in flight, and her way was that which they followed when, in times of drought, the whole group hungered for water.

One old mare died of water famine. That was the only casualty in the band that Mischief led through the summer and the winter, and into the pale green of spring that spread over the desert like a thin mist. She was great with foal of Brandy, long before; and it was fortunate that, as the gentle season came, no horse hunters appeared with it. For the State had put a price on the wild horses, a bounty, as on so many wolves.

By small marches, the herd wandered where the grass was springing and where water flowed at hand. And on a day when the Sierra Blanca stood white indeed under the western sky, and the sun was already beginning to burn with the full promise of the summer's heat, the foal was born that men afterward called "Parade." He was a golden chestnut like his father, Brandy; he was stockinged like him in black silk to the knees and hocks; he had the same sooty muzzle, and, above all, between the eyes, the white sign of his race was printed.

But there were differences, also. Never was there a gentler spirit among horses than Brandy; and never was there a prouder or a fiercer one than that of Parade. When first he stood braced on his long, spindling legs, already his head was high, and his tail arched; already, too, the fire was kindled in his eyes. Mischief, looking him over wisely, knew that she had brought into the world a lord of their kind.

In three days, he could keep up with the galloping herd, and proved it, for on that third day a group of bounty hunters came with racing horses and with crackling guns. For good shooting the reward was fairly high, for the ranchmen were tired of having their saddle stock swept off the range into the band of some wild stallion, to be lost permanently, or else worn out by constant hard traveling. They were striking at the root of the trouble—the stallions themselves. And on this day it was that the buckskin stopped in his stride and squealed with pain.

Parade, looking back, saw the beautiful animal crumble to its knees, then fall flat upon the ground. The wind brought up the sickening odor of blood, and his mother ran beside him, snorting as she ran:

"It's the Great Enemy! It's Man! Whenever men come, there'll be the smell of blood! Look! The pinto mare is down. See how her shoulder is covered with red? The Great Enemy kills from far off. Fly for your life, oh brave, oh noble son of mine!"

Four of the herd were killed on that day, when the band was safe, the long legs of Parade were shaking under him. He lay down in the shadow of his mother, and every staggering beat of his heart thrummed home in his brain the newly learned lessons:

"Man is the Great Enemy! Man kills from afar! With the scent of Man comes the smell of iron and powder, and the latter scent is that of death. There is no wind so cold, there is no sun so hot, as the wrath of Man. Therefore, Man is the Great Enemy."

He would not forget those lessons. Through that summer and that autumn, he had the point brought home to him more than once. If he learned to run as never a horse on the range had run before him, the bullets of men were what gave him wings. The herd dissolved. Half were dead, half were scattered. There remained only Mischief and her foal, lurking in the great wilderness of the Sierra Blanca, in fear of the very ground on which they trod.

"We must go in a straight line, on and on," said Parade to his mother. "There is fear all around us! We must go straight on until we leave it behind us."

She answered: "Fear is a thing that can never be lost, except by slaves. The stupid beasts which wear saddles and carry men in them may be safe, but all the rest of us are afraid. Every wild thing is afraid. Even the wolf goes in fear. The mountain lion sneaks out of its lair to hunt. The grizzly skulks through the brush and hides among the rocks. You want to escape from fear, but it would be easier to escape from yourself. You want to run over the edge of the horizon and find a new world, but all you can ever find is a new skyline. Trouble will rain down on you everywhere out of the brightest heaven. And the wise horse, my son, is he who makes the best of the grass and the water at hand, no matter how far he may have to range for it."

They went into that winter alone, and it was a bitter

36

one. It began with a norther that whitened the desert and the mountains alike. They had to paw through the snow to get at the scanty grass beneath. Then the chinook blew. Dark flags flew from the peaks, and the warm wind melted the snow for a day. Afterward the frost congealed the water to ice, a transparent coat of armor through which hoofs could not break.

Even wild horses would have starved then, but Mischief was wise among her kind, and she showed the colt how to forage in the lee of the bluffs where the chinook had not melted the snow, and where it could still be broken away for the sake of the sparse grass beneath.

They lived, but with death fingering their ribs and looking them in the eye every day. Men had hunted them all through the year until winter; now winter itself reached out for them with hands of ice.

Then the wolves hunted them down the Wainwright Valley. Seven great lobos—gaunt skeletons whose loose hides waved and rippled as they ran, red-eyed, with teeth that shone like ice—hunted the mare and her foal through the narrow pass, and out through the plain, and around in a great circle. For three days, they hung to the trail, far slower of foot than the horses, but patient as hunger itself.

The starving colt would never forget how he ran when his legs were numb, of how his mother, when he staggered, came beside him and nipped him cruelly, hip and flank, wringing his tender flesh with her teeth until the torment spurred him into a stronger gallop.

With snorts and with whinnyings, with half-human moans, she scolded him through the length of that frightful three-day run.

"There's neither heart nor pride in you!" she would say, "and yet you are the son of a king! The blood of a king is in you, but you let a pack of filthy timber wolves run you down! If you were the son of Brandy in spirit as well as the flesh, you'd make the wind whistle so fast for ten minutes that all the skulking flesheaters would give up and stand to howl at the sky."

Those taunts were more to Parade than cruel nippings that drove him forward; and now, for the first time, the picture of his father began to loom in his eyes, growing greater and greater through the time to come, a picture of a horse like a winged, golden flame. Pride and blood kept Parade running through those three days, until the wolves slunk away and their angry voices rang with hollow echoes down a long ravine, to tell that they had surrendered the contest.

Parade would have fallen, but Mischief put her shoulder against him so that he could stand; well she knew that, once down, the ice on the ground and the ice in the wind would soon freeze the blood that ran in her son.

A week after that, the spring came suddenly, and the first great ordeal had ended. It left Parade with a gaunted belly, a roached back, and a coat shaggy and weather-faded. But it left him all hammered steel in body and in spirit.

That year the grass was good, the water holes were freshened by many rains, and Parade grew with wonderful speed. They picked up a few of the wild strays, willing enough to follow the leadership of the wise mare, Mischief; and again the herd was the salvation of the mare and her foal, for when the horse hunters came with their rifles, Mischief and Parade were always first away, and the rifles did their work on the rearmost members of the band.

It was at this same time that the legend began of a young stallion, a mere yearling, that ranged through the Sierra Blanca with the beauty of a golden thunderbolt. That legend grew. Old prospectors forgot their quest when they heard of it; old cattlemen looked with squinted eyes at the picture that formed far off in their minds; and many a boy on the range planned against the future when he might ride a peerless horse.

By winter, the band had been dispersed once more. Again Mischief and Parade went lonely through the season of ice that was beating the colt with white hammers into the metal that was to make him lord of the range.

When he was a two-year-old, men began to hunt him, not with rifles but with relays of fast horses.

A wild hawk flies better than any tame-bred one because it has to live for twenty hours a day on the wing, and Parade was running constantly. No trainer of horses would have dared to work a colt as the hunters in the Sierra Blanca worked that fugitive.

That autumn, Hammersley, the English rancher,

brought up three dozen horses and eight riders, and worked Parade for a month. Mischief had to turn out of the way. He ran for the first time alone; and for a month his keen ears, his blazing eyes, above all, his sense of smell, keener than the nostrils of a wolf, studied all that lay between him and the horizon. And fear crept beside him, rose like a ghost out of the ground, became such a familiar presence that it no longer sapped his strength or filled his lungs with a breath of icy mist. He had been tested a hundred times, and always he had won. Confidence was born. He had the wariness of a grizzly, that wisest animal, but he had the courage of a grizzly, too.

So he endured Hammersley's famous running, about which men will tell you still, yonder in the Sierra Blanca, and wherever celebrated horse hunts are talked about. For a month, Parade stood off every challenge and then was able to leave the dispirited hunters and go free.

They had lost one man, killed instantly by a fall from a mustangs which put its foot into a hole. They lost five horses; three because of broken legs received in the frantic races through the mountains, one through sheer heartbreak of fatigue, and another so worn to the bone that it was not worth while to drag the poor brute out of the desert.

Afterward, legend increased those losses, multiplying them by three. Men said that Hammersley had spent twenty thousand dollars on the hunt. Parade became a lodestar to attract every lover of great horseflesh.

When the Hammersley hunt ended, Parade went up the Wainwright Valley, found his mother and went off with her.

That was only the beginning of things.

Half a dozen outfits tried for Parade the next year. The most celebrated effort was that of Wilton Parker and Champ Rainey, who clung to the task for six weeks, with an army of horses and a small host of expert riders and ropers.

They failed, for Parade had learned and mastered the most difficult lesson of all, which is that a hunted horse must not run in a circle, but in a straight line. They might start him in a curve, and herd him into it for a time, but eventually he recognized the circle and broke away like a hawk across the horizon. Then they had to plan on his

39

probable lines of retreat, and place relays of horses and hunters along them. It was during this year that Joseph C. Curry ran Parade a hundred miles with eleven relays, and killed six good horses on the way, but Parade escaped with a greater fame than ever. And about this time some of the men on the range began to declare that Parade would never be taken. The best brains had been used against him, yet he always escaped, always with greater and greater ease.

Also, half a dozen fine marksmen started out, in the fall of this year, letting it be known that they would attempt to crease the stallion, since he could be captured in no other way. To crease a horse is to shoot a bullet across the nape of the neck, jarring the spinal column sufficient to stun the animal; but for one horse captured in this way, a hundred are killed. And Sheriff Tom Crawford published far and wide the fact that with his own rifle he would "crease" the man who shot the famous stallion dead. The creasing experts, at that, gave up their attempt.

Parade's name was known far and wide by this time. Newspapers had taken him up as front page material. Travelers from distant lands begged to be brought within eyeshot of the famous horse. But even this was becoming more and more difficult. He and Mischief had learned how to hide themselves like foxes; they had learned the value of making hundred-mile marches from one good grazing place to another.

And then calamity began. It was not the fault of Parade, but the weakness of Michief, that brought the final great trouble on them in the same year when Parade began to be called the "Hundred-thousand-dollar Horse."

CHAPTER VII

THE GREAT ENEMY

That winter was given a spark of excitement by poor Hammersley's second great attempt to catch the golden stallion whose beauty had become a devouring fire of his mind. Hammersley was being ruined by his prolonged horse hunting. It was not so much the money he spent on the task as the way his ranch went to ruin during his absences, for everyone he trusted was taking advantage of the placid, good-natured Englishman. Hammersley hunted Parade for three furious weeks of effort, during the cold season, only to find that his well-shod horses could do no better over the frozen ground than could the bare hoofs of the stallion. Mischief, as usual, was simply shunted to the side, and the hunt flew past her, but Parade could not be taken.

In the spring, Parker and Joe Curry combined. They tried a new project, which was to starve Parade with a water famine by fencing off all of the water holes over a considerable district, using tough barbed wire for the task. When the holes were fenced, Curry and Parker made the rounds eagerly and found three of the fences broken down in a singular manner. The horses had not been able to handle the barbed wire, of course, but they had worked at the slender posts, usually of crooked mesquite wood, until one or two of the posts went down. Then the fence was soon flat.

Once Mischief and her son learned the system, a barbed wire fence was no more than a trifle to them, unless the posts were big and sunk deep in firm ground. So that laborious effort on the part of Curry and Parker became history, and the legend of the golden stallion grew more formidable than ever. The time had come when tens of thousands of ardent sympathizers prayed that the great horse would never be captured. And at that very time, trouble was preparing for Parade, a mysterious and unexpected danger.

It came about in this way. He and Mischief had gone to the northern limits of the range of the Sierra Blanca, not by chance, but because they were taken with a longing for the grass which grew rank and heavy on the slopes of the hills that reached like fingers into the desert. Here were scrub trees, too, and masses of shrubbery whose green tips made delectable provender to the tough palates of the desert-bred horses. Sometimes the pair ventured to remain among those pleasant foothills for as much as a a week at a time, though as a rule caution made them change their place of residence after a two- or three-day halt.

They had come up off the sands to relish this earthly paradise; in half an hour they had cropped an abundant meal of the long, rather salty grass. They had drunk deep at a rivulet of cold, pure water, and then began to pluck at the green, tender sprouts that tipped the branches. Mischief lifted her wise head, after a few moments, and snorted.

"Do you find that scent in the air?" she asked.

"I do," said Parade. "As foul as a dead body; nothing but a buzzard could like it!"

"Yes, a buzzard," said Mischief, "or the Great Enemy, or a bear."

"The Enemy?" said Parade. "Will Man like such a thing as that?"

"All meat eaters are foul," said the mare, "and even if you know very little about the matter, you understand that Man is a meat eater."

"That is true," said Parade, "but I can't understand it."

"You are young, my son," said Mischief, looking over the bronze and rippling strength of the stallion, "and you must learn that that which is not understood is always strange, but the horse of much understanding is the lord of the herd. The horse that cannot understand, at least should be silent. There was your father, Parade. He was a king of horses. I shall never see his like again. But he understood that it was best in everything to defer to my experience, and that was why he led the herd gloriously for the time he was with it. As for understanding that Man could enjoy such a scent as that one yonder, let me tell you the fact. Man himself puts out those horrible odors in order to attract the four-footed meat eaters—wolves and bears. I have smelled it before, and there is always a trap near it!"

She began to work cautiously up the wind, with Parade moving beside her, a little to the rear. Now that age had dulled the edge of her speed, she liked nothing better than to show off her superior experience. She moved like a cat, her knees bending with readiness to spring to one side or the other. And Parade kept one bright eye on her movements, the other on the ground they passed over.

Presently, she paused.

"There's the bush that the smell has been put on by

Man. What a stench! And somewhere near us there is sure to be a trap."

She pawed lightly at the sand in front of her. A bright thing leaped up out of the ground. A huge mouth had opened, and powerful teeth clanked together—a jaw without body or head, a very incarnation of evil!

The thing lay still on the ground, now. Parade had covered a hundred yards in the twinkling of an eye, but the whinny of his mother called him back. He came prancing and dancing, feathering himself on tiptoe.

"That is the trap," said the mare calmly. As a matter of fact, she was trembling inwardly with excitement, thinking how close that terrible engine had come to her foot.

"Mother," said Parade, "there is more courage in you than in a whole herd, and more wisdom in you than in twenty old mares whom time has eaten away like the mange."

"Well, well," said Mischief contentedly, "there is very little wisdom in the management of this world, I fear, but after all, I dare say that it is wisdom that makes courage bright. Not that I should be saying such things of myself. But it is a cruel pupil that denies credit to a teacher, and experience has taught me, my son. There is a sample of the work of the Great Enemy. You can see what it would do."

"It would smash the leg of a wolf. It must be meant for a bear," said Parade, snuffing at the thing from a distance, staring at it with his great, bright eyes.

"Yes, for a bear," said Mischief. "And one day a bear would have stepped into it, perhaps, and then there would have been a crashing and smashing and a roaring and snarling, until the hills trembled."

"I would like to see such a thing," said Parade. "The cunning devils have eaten enough horseflesh!"

"Aye," said the mare. "There is a living brain in the forefoot of a grizzly. It is delicate enough to pick a small grub out of rotten wood; but it is also strong enough to smash in the ribs of a grown horse. Well, if men are near enough to have set this trap, it is time for us to leave this place."

She started to swing around.

"Back up! Back up!" exclaimed Parade. "Put down your hoofs where you stepped before or—"

"So?" said Mischief angrily. "Has the time come when you are to start teaching your mother what—"

The ground seemed to lift to meet her right forefoot, as she spoke. She sprang back on three legs; to the fourth clung a naked pair of iron jaws like that which already had been snapped shut. But this time the trap had closed with only a horrible crunching sound.

Mischief did not struggle, but a sweat of agony spotted her neck and her flanks. She bowed her head and sniffed at the engine that clutched her. Behind the jaws appeared a heavy chain, lying snakelike upon the ground.

"Go, my son," said the mare. "They have taken me now."

"I shall never leave you," said Parade, all dark and shining in a moment with sweat. "I shall stay here—"

"And be caught with a rope and be turned into a slave?" exclaimed Mischief. "As for me, I am old. I have no great time left to me. Besides, this is only a right judgment. I have been proud, and, therefore, I was blind. Age ought to kill pride before it kills the body, but I have remained as high-headed as a young filly in her second spring. Parade, leave me. Will it be a comfort to me to pass under the saddle and bridle again and know that you are suffering with me? What? You haven't felt spurs! Listen to me and don't be a fool."

A quiet rustling approached them, no louder than the small sound of a wind that walks among green leaves. From among the shrubbery appeared the clumsy body of a grizzly bear, with a vast rounded head, and the wrinkles of wisdom cut deep between the eyes.

Mischief, with a groan of fear, lunged back. The long chain rattled out its length and then held firm. The mare sank on her haunches.

"My son!" she neighed.

Parade sprang before her. He seemed ready to hurl himself at that formidable monster, that creature made for war.

The grizzly stood up with its paws held together, very like a prize fighter stuffing his hands deeper into the gloves.

"A little closer, my son," growled the bear, and his red eyes shifted in his head. A drool of saliva dripped from a corner of his mouth.

44

"Away from him!" commanded the mare. "He looks clumsy, but he can charge like a rock jumping down hill, and with one stroke he can smash in your skull!"

Parade drew back, slowly, unwillingly.

The bear dropped forward on all fours, with a rolling motion, at once wonderfully clumsy and with the grace of infinite strength.

"Horse meat," said the grizzly, "is good for a working bear. This bit looks old and tough, but there will be a few tender places along the back. And if a fool has a soft heart, then hers should make good eating!"

He waddled closer to Mischief. With a dull eye of despair, she saw destruction approaching. Parade, in futile agony, galloped around and around them, while a cloud of dust rolled upward toward the sky. All that ground might be sowed with traps, but in his frenzy he forgot. If he could dart in and strike with his forehoofs—but he knew that the paws of the grizzly were a subtle pair of thunderbolts from which he could not escape.

Mischief lurched to her feet, suddenly, as though she wished to take her death standing.

"And what a fool you were," said the grizzly, "to walk on ground where a bear feared to tread. But it will soon be over now. There is one lesson that every fool must learn, in the end, and that's the lesson that I'm about to teach you. This is a lucky day. I've almost forgotten horse meat —and here it is in a fine lump for me! I would rather have a colt half your size, madame, but I shan't look a gift horse in the mouth."

"Parade! Away!" neighed the mare suddenly. "They're coming from behind you."

The stallion looked back, and he saw three riders galloping straight at him over the ridge of the hill. Terror sent him away in a bright golden streak.

Behind him, he saw the grizzly scuttling off with a speed wonderful for such a loosely jointed body. He heard the rifles clang like sledge-hammers beating together, face to face. He saw the bear halt, turn, and charge in. He saw it pause again, and slump slowly to the ground. Then the dust of his own raising veiled the picture from the eyes of Parade.

He ran on, and he ran alone. He would run forever

45

alone, he felt. The Sierra Blanca became suddenly more lofty and more vast, and he shrank to a lonely speck that crawled aimlessly across it and trailed behind a little wisp of dust.

CHAPTER VIII

REUNION

IT WAS DAVE LARCHMONT, CATTLE KING, HORSE BREEDER, and great hunter, who took the pelt off the dead grizzly, and then led Mischief limping to his ranch. It looked as though that torn foreleg would never heal properly, and he would have killed the mare, but he had recognized that streak of golden lightning which had dashed away from the scene. The mother of Parade was worth having, even if she could only stand on three legs. If she could give the world one foal like the famous stallion, might she not give another, and another?

He took Mischief back to his ranch, not far from Parmalee, and straightway his place was deluged with visitors. They came in floods, with cameras. The corral where Mischief stood was constantly surrounded. Not that she filled the eye more than many other horses, but because an aroma, a glamour of great romance, clung to this mother of Parade, this companion of his many adventures.

Her wound healed. She could walk, trot, canter, and even run, but at every gait she limped, and she would always limp. The tendons had been frayed by the steel teeth of the trap, and now they were drawn a vital bit shorter.

Big Harry Richmond, fatter of body, more like a great blue crane than ever, came and stared at her, and with him came Charlie Moore. He was close to sixty now, but it was not the passing of the years that had suddenly turned his hair white. Grief had done it, and the knowledge that he was still bound inexorably to Richmond.

"It's comin' close to the end, Charlie," said Richmond. "Now they've got Mischief, they'll be gettin' hold of Parade one of these days. And there'll be a lot of whoopin' then. Larchmont," he said to the other rancher, "look at the way she's marchin' up and down that fence, lookin' out at the evenin' as it comes over the hills. You reckon she's lookin' for Parade, too? You reckon that he might show up, one of these days?"

Larchmont shrugged his shoulders.

"You been hearin' a lot of talk about that Parade horse," he said. "You got him all built up. Think he'd have the sense to come all the way down here from the Sierra Blanca? Even if he had the sense, think he'd have the nerve? No, sir, that Parade knows enough to be scared of men, and he's goin' to stay on his own campin' grounds, where he knows the howl of every wolf and the hoot of every owl. He ain't no miracle horse, Richmond."

But that same evening, Parade came over the naked hills toward Parmalee.

He moved like a soldier who has passed inside the lines of the enemy; and, in fact, all around him there were signs of the Great Enemy, and the scent of iron was never out of his nostrils. Half a dozen times, before this, he had ventured farther and farther over the trail by which Mischief had been taken from his ken. He knew how it pointed, and now he was determined to follow it to the end.

But every step was a mighty peril to him. On the trail there was the smell of iron from the hoofs of shod horses. Iron again breathed at him, new or rusted, from the fences. And through the air came the scent of such food as the flesh eaters could relish, mingled with smoke, and again the poisonous breath of hot iron.

There was iron everywhere. The stain of it filled the air. And then again he would pass a huge barn, a dark blotchy outline in the distance, out of which the wind carried to him such fragrances as must be found in the heaven of horses: the sweetness of sun-cured hay, and delights that Parade could guess at but could not know.

He went on at a trot or a swinging lope, most of the time, only slowing to a walk when the way led too close to a dwelling of man. And so he came across the hollow and up to the horse corral of Dave Larchmont.

There were full thirty head of mares and young colts in

that corral now. Mischief stayed there alone, during the day, in order that the curious might satisfy their eyes by gazing upon her; but at night, all the best of the grazing saddle stock was herded back to this place of security. Dave Larchmont had invested many thousands of dollars in working up that nucleus of a saddle string which was to be the delight and wonder of the range. He could not afford to let horses worth five hundred a throw wander abroad, where careless fellows might "borrow" them here and there.

He penned them up at night, and let one cowpuncher ride night herd over them.

Parade, from the deep darkness of the hollow, saw that rider pass and repass, and his strength of will loosened in him. He studied the wind that blew to him from the crowd in the corral, but there were too many conflicting scents for him to pick out Mischief from the lot. Only a premonition, an instinct, warned him that she might be there.

He whinnied. It was a mere whicker, a shadowy whisper of sound. Out of the entangled shadows of the corralled horses, it brought one form that moved rapidly up and down the line of the fence.

Now he knew for certain that Mischief was there. The rider passed. He paused on the farther side of the corral to roll a cigarette, and as he smoked, he sang, softly, as a good puncher will do when he rides night herd; and as he sang, he looked toward the yellow-lighted window through which the murmuring voices of his companions drifted, as they sat at their poker game. Chance can play cruel tricks, but none so evil as when it sends out into the night a fellow who has plenty of money in his wallet when a poker game is at hand!

Parade, in the meantime, went up the slope like a great cat, with the stars striking dull sparks out of his lustrous coat. Mischief followed him down the inner side of the fence. There were eight feet of that fence, and the bars were close, until they came to the gate, which was built of far lighter stuff, so that it could be handled more easily. Not because it was a gate, but because the bars here were farther apart, Parade paused, and thrust his head between them, and touched the tremulous muzzle of Mischief.

"Be quiet—hush! There is a man on guard," said Mischief. "And he carries a gun, which you know about, and a rope, also. He will be at you like a mountain lion, if he guesses that you are here. Oh, my son, I have told the others that you would come. It is terribly rash of you, but love is greater than mountains and stronger than rivers. What have you done since I left you?"

"I have been alone," said Parade. "I have been alone in the desert, afraid of shadows that seemed to be dropping out of the sky. The Sierra Blanca is ten times as great as before, and I am ten times as small. How has it been with you?"

"I am lamed," said Mischief. "I can run, but not as I ran before. Men come every day and look at me. They speak a great deal in the voices which we cannot understand. I am sad, but now I must pay for my pride and folly."

A tall colt with a great white blaze on his forehead came curiously toward them.

"Go back!" commanded Mischief, swinging toward the interloper.

As the mare swung away from him, Parade pressed harder against the gate to come nearer to her. The wood creaked and groaned. A sudden sense of the weakness of that barrier ran tingling to his brain. One thrust might down the gate; one effort might set the door wide for his mother.

The guard had heard the sound.

"Halloo! Halloo!" he called. "Steady, boys! Don't crowd that gate, you fools!"

He started his horse at a gallop, and came swinging around the corral. Parade could see the hat and the head sailing past the horizon stars.

Should he recoil, and bound down the slope of loosened rock? He snorted with the desperation of fear and hope commingled, and with one thrust of his shoulder he burst the fragile lock of the gate. It swung in, and before Parade himself had recovered, Mischief was through the gap. Not she alone, but the tall colt with the white blaze followed, and Parade, as he turned and shot down the slope, sent his mighty neighing blowing like a red flag to call the others.

They came, for in that neigh there was the promise of freedom, the defiance of masters, the whole band of Dave

49

Larchmont's chosen horses burst through the gateway and hustled down the slope after their leader.

Right at them, from the flank, charged the guard.

He had drawn a revolver and was firing it repeatedly into the air to give the alarm. His wild shouts rang back to the house, and brought the other punchers in a fury of haste.

But they were far too late. By the time they had saddled their commoner horseflesh from the other corral, the stream of the liberated was pouring far off toward the Sierra Blanca.

The cowpuncher vainly spurred behind them. He was able to overtake Mischief, but what was she, compared with the fortune in horseflesh which was streaming away into the night? Desperately he rode, but when the dawn came, he had merely succeeded in tracing the fugitives to the edge of the desert.

There he paused because his mustang was exhausted. And far off to the north of him, Mischief jogged contentedly on. She knew where to find her son, and in the Wainwright Valley, sure enough, she discovered him before noon of that day, with such a herd gathered around him as never another wild stallion ever was lord over.

Up and down ranged Parade, eying his new possessions, mastering them with a kingly eye, and keeping a wary lookout for the dangers that would surely come rolling over the horizon before long. When Mischief came, he went to greet her, and they moved together up and down.

He exulted: "Men are not the great masters, after all. They can be met. They can be beaten. *I* have beaten them, mother!"

She quaked as though a strong wind had cut at her.

"You saw how they put teeth in the ground, teeth that will bite though there is nobody behind them? Ah, well, there would be no fools, except that they rejoice in their folly! My son, I have told you of the danger in the tooth of the rattlesnake, and the wiles by which a wolf will hamstring the greatest stallion in the world, and the cunning of a hawk in the air, and the wisdom of an otter in a stream filled with fish, but now I tell you that all of these are nothing compared with man. I have felt his hot iron burn into my skin. Twice he has reached into the wild desert and taken me. Will you still be a fool and rejoice in your folly?"

For answer, Parade neighed loud and long.

Every head among the stolen horses snapped up from the grazing; every eye shone with new brightness, turning toward the master.

"Do you see?" said Parade. "They are mine! And they can run over the ground like birds gliding down the sky. When the horse hunters come, how will they be able to catch such horses as these, with your wits to give us the warning, and my heels to show the herd the proper way? We have been wandering like foolish little hunted things. Now we can live like lords of the earth!"

CHAPTER IX

THE RODEO RACE

It was not long after this, far south from the Sierra Blanca, far south from Parmalee, that the horses lined up for a rodeo race. There was not much of a purse to be run for, but the betting was high. Nearly every cowpuncher in that section of the country had put up all he had; guns had been sold and spurs pawned to raise cash, and all around the little half-mile track there were tense spectators.

A dozen horses had lined up for the start. There was a long, low mare from the Indian country, and she had her share of betting; there was a dappled gray out of the Pecos region, a picture-horse that made many a cowpuncher reach for his wallet; and among the rest there was a brown stallion, rather time-worn, his hip bones thrusting up at sharp angles. Nevertheless, at least half the money had been bet on him, for that was Brandy and on his back was the meager body and the ape-like face of Lake, the half-breed.

Upon Lake and the stallion, one man stared with a peculiar intensity of interest. He forgot the race impending, he forgot the fluttering flags, he forgot the lowing of cattle in the distance. Suddenly the sun seemed to press on him with a greater heat. He took off his sombreo to wipe his face, and showed the features of a man who might be anywhere from twenty-five to thirty years of age, with a spot of gray hair over each temple. As he settled the hat back on his head, a man near him said:

"What you pick, stranger? My money's on the gray. I never seen such a hoss."

"If looks could win, he has the race before it starts," agreed Silvertip. "But looks won't beat Brandy—not if he gets an honest ride."

"Honest ride?" said the other. "You think that that half-breed would—"

The starting gun tore that sentence off short. The yell of the cowpunchers seemed to strike the sky and fly back from it in echoes. Madness of joy and hope set the watchers dancing. Only Silvertip remained aloof from the excitement, with the faint smile touching the corners of his mouth and his glance wandering calmly from face to face of the spectators, with hardly a glance at the racers.

The old melancholy had suddenly dropped on him in the midst of all this turmoil. These were men who wanted to win. To lose their money would be almost like losing their blood. Their eyes were wolfish, their nostrils flared. They struck at the air with their fists, or with open hands they pulled on invisible wires to draw their favorites forward in the race.

But Silvertip stood outside of all this. He had put down fifty dollars on Brandy as a mere gesture. He had a little silver outside of that sum, and that was all. But he was still more interested in the people than in the race. And, as he glanced from man to man, he was wishing with all his might that he could commit himself so utterly to a moment and lose every other thought.

It was a good moment for Silver, in a sense, for he was able to probe deeply into the minds around him, while they were regardless of his eyes; it was an evil moment in that it made him realize, more than ever, the strange gulf that separated him from other men. And suddenly he told himself, through his teeth, that if he could not gain an interest in any other way, he would resort to crime. There, at least, one could be assured of sufficient excitement to stir the blood.

People began to shout the name of Brandy. Silver saw

that the field had completed the first round of the track and that they were well along the second and last lap, with Brandy running second to the gray stallion from the Pecos. Easily the long strides of Brandy covered the ground; he seemed to slide along as though he were the shadow trailed by a kite.

But in spite of the ease of his striding, he did not gain on the gray. And now the mare, the long, low-built mare, came streaking up on the outside. The stallion drew ahead. The gray and the mare fought nose to nose, while Brandy dropped gradually back.

A wail of dismay broke upward from the crowd; when men groan, they lift their heads.

"He's too old; he's worn out; Brandy's done for!" men were saying around Silvertip, but Silvertip knew better.

He had seen the pull of the half-breed, something more than that weight on the reins which steadies a horse and helps it to stretch out to full speed. Now the whip flashed into Lake's hand. It rose and fell methodically, while with his left hand Lake jerked at the reins. One would have thought that he was working with all his might to get the utmost out of Brandy, but the keen eye of Silvertip saw that those pulls on the reins were exactly timed to unbalance the stridings of Brandy. More rapidly he fell to the rear. Four horses in a cluster swept up and past him.

And then a dull heat began near the heart of Silvertip. It spread through his body. It flushed his face. It burned in his brain. This was not the first time that he had seen Lake at one crooked trick or another, but to cheat a horse seemed much more horrible than to cheat a man.

The gray stallion and the mare, still running head to head, rounded into the stretch. A furlong off, down the straightaway, was the finish, and both riders went to the whip.

Far, far back, was Brandy, but coming again as if with a second wind—a cunning trick on the part of Lake to give himself a chance honestly to ride out a horse that he himself had hopelessly beaten in the course of the running.

A yell ripped into the ear of Silvertip, the harsh, sudden outcry of many astonished men. Something had happened, and it was to Brandy. The right-hand rein had broken away at the bit, and, no longer troubled by the pull of his jockey, Brandy came up the track as if on wings. He rounded the sharp corner at the head of the stretch, swinging wide to clear the cluster of horses which was struggling there.

They fell behind. The track seemed to flow back against them, carrying them to the rear. Only Brandy it allowed to speed ahead.

Lake was no longer using his whip. It would have been like flogging an avalanche.

But far away, the gray stallion and the long mare were fighting toward the finish. Now the head of the gray began to bob. The mare shot ahead. Victory brightened the eyes of her rider.

Then the thundering of the crowd gave him warning as the chorus shouted for Brandy. There came the stallion on the outside, with enormous strides. The rider of the mare yelled with fear. The mare strained to her utmost under the rapid cutting of the whip. Very different was that picture from the sight of Lake, clinging to his place with a distorted face, one hand twisted into the flying mane of the stallion.

They seemed to strike the finish line at the same instant, though Brandy was immediately half a length ahead before the pair began to ease up. Perhaps that was what influenced the judges, and the name of Brandy was posted as winner.

The favorite had won, and so had Silvertip, but he collected his bet with an abstracted air. Drifting to the verge of the group that was packed around Brandy, he heard Lake explaining in a sullen voice:

"He kind of sulked. He dodged it all the way through the start. Then he got hold and run away on me. I never seen such a fool hoss."

How much had Lake and Harry Richmond stood to win by pulling Brandy in that race—wondered Silvertip. What had been the life of the fine horse during these years? Unless he was very much mistaken in horseflesh, long ago Brandy's name should have been among the winners of some of the great Eastern stakes; but still he seemed unknown, except in the pickup races of Western rodeos and fairs.

Silver drifted with the crowd, afterward. He was not a part of the rejoicing. All life seemed flat and savorless to him. The only fire that burned in him was one of steady horror that such a horse as Brandy should be in such hands as those of the half-breed and the crooked rancher, Richmond.

Silvertip was not drinking. He was merely wandering with the crowd, preoccupied. He had one pleasant surety, which was that in this place he would not be recognized. But even in that he was wrong, for a man with a square, lined face came up to him and tapped him on the arm.

"My name's Dodgson," said he. "I'm the sheriff of this county. I know you, Silvertip, and I wanta say that I'm watchin' you. If there's any gun play in *this* town, self-defense ain't goin' to be worth anything for you to talk about."

He gave Silvertip a glimpse of his badge, and went on.

Silvertip, in disgust, turned into the first big saloon and took a whisky at the bar. Men were crowding up to the rail. Voices were shouting. Half of that crowd was already drunk, and their jolly condition seemingly was envied by the other half. But the liquor was no more than a sourness in the throat of Silver, a foul smoke in his brain.

He passed on into the big back room where a dozen groups sat at the tables, playing poker; the half-breed, Lake, was at one of them. The sight of him made the jaw muscles of Silvertip bulge. He came near, but not too near. He saw the progress of the game at once, and that all the flow of money was toward Lake. In ten minutes, one of the men pushed back his chair and slammed down the cards with such violence that one of them skidded into the air and dropped near the feet of Silver. The latter picked it up.

"It's no good," said he who had risen. "I've seen more cards here than I ever seen before in a whole night, but I can't win. It ain't my day, and I'm licked and busted. So long, boys!"

"Wait a minute," said the voice of Silvertip.

He approached, holding the blue-backed card which had fallen to the floor. On the back of it was what he had expected—a faint blue smudge, almost indistinguishable to an inexperienced eye, and located half way between one corner of the card and the center of it. The card itself was a jack, and it was not hard to guess that every honor card in the pack had been similarly marked by Lake, by this

55

time. Perhaps the entire pack was tampered with, and to the half-breed it would be as if the faces of the other hands were turned toward him.

"Wait for what?" asked the man who had left the game.

Lake, twisting about in his chair, saw Silvertip and turned a yellow-green. Fascinated, he watched while Silver threw the card back onto the table.

"Wait for Lake," said Silvertip. "You don't want to carry the joke any further than this, Lake," he added. And to the other bewildered players he went on. "He takes a hand with the boys, now and then, but nobody ever loses through him."

"What's all this lingo mean?" demanded a fiery youth at the table.

"It means that Lake is shoving back the pile he's won, and leaving the game," said Silver. "That's all. Take your table stakes, and come along with me, Lake."

He saw the lips of the half-breed twist away from yellow teeth, but no words came. Then, selecting one stack of coins, Lake dropped them into his pocket, and stood up. His eyes were fighting those of Silvertip every instant.

"Is this gent a crook?" asked the youth of the party. "Is that why you're hooking him away, big boy?"

But Silver gave no answer.

"Walk ahead of me," he commanded Lake. "Go out the back door, and don't try to get away. The spots are still on that pack of cards. I suppose you've still got the crayons on you. And if I split your wishbone for you, nobody will care a bit."

CHAPTER X

SILVERTIP'S DISCOVERY

THEY STOOD BETWEEN THE BACK OF THE SALOON AND A woodshed, with a pair of dusty-leaved cactus plants near by. Lake was shaking like a bulldog that wants to hurl itself at a jungle tiger, despite all differences of size and fighting talents. But if the red fury was in his eyes, the green sickness of terror was in his face. The greatness of his emotion made his voice and his entire body tremble.

"There was twenty thousand bucks in that game," he groaned. "I could 'a' had the whole of it. It was the best chance that I ever had, and I could 'a' had the whole of it! I'm goin' to have the heart out of you, for this!"

"Why don't I march you back inside?" demanded Silvertip, looking Lake over calmly. "Why don't I take you back inside and show the boys the smudges on the backs of those cards?"

The half-breed was silent. But as he breathed, his nostrils kept working in and out like the nostrils of a panting horse, and the muscles of his ugly, frog-like face kept pulling at, and distorting his features.

"I brought you out here to get some information out of you," said Silvertip. "The last I saw of you, you were trying to steal Brandy. How does that happen?"

"Ask Harry Richmond," snarled Lake.

Silvertip smiled at him, and then made a cigarette. It was very dangerous business, for Lake had been tormented to the point of madness, and as he saw both the hands of Silver occupied, his own hands jumped and jerked several times in the direction of the guns that he wore under his coat. Yet something held him back; an invisible thread bound his strength and kept him helpless; with every moment the mastery of Silvertip grew more complete.

He was saying: "I won't ask Richmond. I'm asking you. What happened after Brandy got away?"

"Richmond hunted him, and old Charlie Moore caught him."

"Charlie still owns half the horse?"

"No. He gave up his half because Richmond made a big job gettin' Brandy back."

"Richmond made the big job of it, and Charlie caught the horse, eh?"

"Yeah. That's it."

"What did Charlie get out of it?"

"He got a chance to groom Brandy every day and talk baby talk to him, and feed him, and set on the edge of the manger and rub his nose."

"That's what he got out of it?"

"Yeah. He's a fool. But that ain't my business."

"What happened to Brandy then?"

"I took him East, and we put him into a coupla races."

"*You* took him East? Then Richmond arranged with you to try to steal him, before that?"

"I dunno nothin' about that," said Lake sullenly.

The eyes of Silvertip shrank to points of brightness.

"Did Brandy win his races?" he asked presently.

"Yeah. He won a coupla. He was goin' good."

"What happened then?"

"He got off his feed, or somethin'. He quit winnin'."

"He couldn't win at all?"

"The dirty crooks, they went and double-crossed us! They throwed Richmond and me and Brandy clean off the tracks. Just when we were ready to haul in the big dough, they ruled us off."

"Because you pulled Brandy in a race?" suggested Silvertip. "Because you bet against him, and pulled him in a race, eh?"

"He was off his feed," muttered Lake.

The faint smile of Silver twisted at one corner of his mouth only. "You threw away your big chance, eh?" said he. "You wanted the quick money—the dirty money. You got one taste of it, and you threw away your chance of the long green, and you threw away Brandy's chance of becoming a famous horse. Ever since that time, you've been dodging around the country, racing Brandy under different names at little rodeos and country fairs. Is that the story?"

"You think you know everything," growled Lake. "What's the good of me tryin' to tell you anything?"

"What a dirty, sneaking lot you are!" said Silvertip calmly. "Where's Moore now?"

"I dunno where the old fool is. Somewhere singin', I guess, because Brandy won the race."

"He wouldn't have won if you'd had your way," observed Silvertip. "I suppose you and Richmond lost a good deal of coin today, betting against your horse?"

The face of Lake worked. He made no other answer.

"And where would Charlie be?" insisted Silvertip.

"I dunno. Out in the sheds at the rodeo grounds, maybe, coolin' off Brandy. Always takes the old fool two or three hours to cool off Brandy after a race. Cool him off and rub him down. You'd think that old skate was a pack of diamonds, the way Charlie works over him."

That was why Silvertip went back to his horse, mounted, and returned to the rodeo grounds. Everyone else had left. It was nearly sunset, and the golden waves of light that rolled across the earth showed only the white head of Charlie Moore, as he walked back and forth, followed by Brandy.

There was no halter on the stallion, but he kept his head close to the left shoulder of his handler all the time. Now that the saddle was off him, he seemed to Silvertip older and more timeworn than ever. Still, he was a horse in ten thousand, with a certain lordliness about even his walking gait.

When Charlie Moore saw Silver, he cried out in a loud voice, and came running; the stallion trotted softly behind him. A moment later, Silver was on the ground, shaking hands.

"All these here years—doggone my soul!" said Charlie Moore. "Where you been, Silvertip?"

"I've been here and there," said Silver.

"I know," said Moore. "We get rumors and whispers, now and then. It ain't newspaper stuff. But sometimes we run into a gent that starts talkin' about a big gent that he knew, somewhere down in Mexico, or up in Alaska, or off in the South Seas, or down in Nicaragua, say. And he'll tell a terrible yarn about what the big gent done, and then he'll say there's a coupla gray spots in his hair."

"That's a lot of talk," said Silvertip. "I've been hearing from Lake a little of what you and Brandy have been through."

The face of Moore darkened.

"He could 'a' been a great stake hoss, Silver," he said huskily. "He could 'a' been one to have his picture in the papers, for a coupla years, and when he was retired to a stud farm, he would 'a' had visitors comin' to see him. He oughta be in a fine green pasture all to himself, and he oughta be eatin' the best oats, and nothin' to do for himself but pose for a camera, now and then. But they throwed him away, Silvertip. They throwed him away."

"He was ruled off, eh?" said Silver.

"It was at Aqueduct," said Charlie Moore. "He'd won a coupla times. The wise gents was watchin' him. They

59

was timin' his moves in trainin'. Tips was beginnin' to float around about him. There was a kind of whisper in the air that a great hoss was on the track. And those crooks didn't want that—Lake and Richmond. They wanted to bring him on slow. They wanted to enter him in some big stake with long odds agin' him, and then they'd clean up and make a fortune. So they decided that they'd spoil his reputation by puttin' him in an overnight race and pullin' him. And they pulled him, all right.

"I ain't goin' to forget how I stood there and watched from the rail, and seen Brandy try to eat up that field and swaller it, and how Lake pulled him double and jammed him into a pocket, and brought him around on the outside, and jammed him into another pocket. And then he came again, with the bit in his teeth. And even the way he was rode, the winner only beat him by a head. And the stewards throwed the whole lot of us off the track. We couldn't race no more anywhere in the country, on a regular track. And since then, we been a lot of bums, travelin' from place to place. Lake handles us, and Richmond sends down a flock of money, now and then, to bet."

He turned away from Silvertip, a little, and let his hand wander over the face of the thoroughbred.

"We won today," said Moore, "but you seen how. And Richmond is goin' to be crazy mad. He must 'a' lost three or four thousand, because he bet agin' us."

He sighed, and added: "Where you bound now, Silver?"

"For the Sierra Blanca," said Silvertip. "I want to take a look at that Parade horse."

"There's a lot that's had a look at him, but there ain't any that's had a hand on him. There ain't goin' to be any, either. Not even you, Silver, I reckon, because now they're huntin' for him with guns."

"Guns?" cried Silvertip. "Hunting for him with guns, did you say?"

"He run off with the fine saddle stock of Dave Larchmont. Ain't you heard about that? There was ten or twelve thousand dollars' worth of stock in that outfit. They started chasin' him to get those hosses back. Dave has worked hard, but he runs more hosses to death than he catches. He caught up eight of 'em, at last, and he took 'em down and corraled 'em with Steve Barrett's hosses.

60

"And in the middle of the night, Parade come and busted down the fence, like he done at Larchmont's place, and he run off with Larchmont's nags, and all of Barrett's too, and they say he's got seventy head of good stock with him out there in the Sierra Blanca, now. Well, ranchers ain't goin' to stand for losses like that, so now they've put a thousand dollars on the scalp of Parade, and the boys are out with their rifles—bad luck to 'em!"

"It's not possible!" said Silvertip. "Nobody would do it. Not even for a thousand dollars. Why, Charlie, it's not in the game—it's not in the cards! Look here! Men started driving that horse—men started hunting him—they drove him for years—and now he's finding out how to hit back—and you mean to tell me they're going to use guns on him?"

Moore nodded. "There's gents alive," he said, "that would cut off an arm for a thousand bucks in cold cash. Don't you make no mistake about it! And they'll have the scalp of Parade, right enough."

"It's murder," said Silvertip quietly.

"Aye," said Charlie. "Murder pays pretty big, if you know the right gents to kill!"

That was how Silvertip started for the Sierra Blanca as fast as a good horse could take him.

When he reached Parmalee, he found talk of very little else in the air. All was news of the last outfits that were to try their hands at capturing the great stallion, or of the hunters who were going out singly, expert shots who carried high-power rifles to end the career of the horse.

Silvertip carried a rifle himself, but it was not to be used on horses, when he rode into the white-and-purple land of the Sierra Blanca.

He rode for four days, and then what he wanted to see came suddenly on his vision. He had hobbled his horse and slept out on a tarpaulin in the hollow corner of a small ravine, and he was wakened about dawn by the sound of hoofs thrumming rapidly over the ground, beating up musical echoes almost like the swift fingering of a tambourine.

So he sat up and saw for the first time in his life a sight that made his heart rush out in an ecstasy of delight. For there was a whole river of horses pouring down the ravine, and at their head ran a creature made of golden

61

fire, a thing of blinding beauty. His trot kept the tide of horses at a gallop; when he swung into a flowing gallop, the others had to race to keep up. It seemed to Silvertip that the stallion barely touched the ground with his hoofs; it seemed to him that there was a beat of invisible wings, supporting and prolonging the striding of that monster. It was not by size but by magnificence that he dwarfed the retinue that poured behind him.

And afterward, when they were gone, Silver remained for a long time, staring before him. He had seen a kingly thing. All his being flowed outward with a desire to possess it.

This was what he had been searching for all his life, one object which he could desire with all his might. Battles with other men had not given him the ultimate thrill, the full madness of joy. In all his days he never had set his hands upon an object utterly capable of filling his heart. And now, at last, he had found it.

When he thought back to the picture that he had seen, it seemed to Silvertip that there had been only one horse running down the valley like a creature of molded flame, and behind the stallion had run futile little shadows.

He stood up and looked his own horse in the eye. It was a good, tough gelding, but it looked to Silvertip like a worthless rag of horseflesh.

He glanced around him at the immensity of the mountains. He felt that the game was lost before he commenced to play it. For that very reason, his heart swelled, and he set his teeth for the great endeavor.

CHAPTER XI

DESERT MEETING

SILVERTIP RODE SIXTY MILES THE NEXT DAY. TWICE HE came within rifle shot of the horse herd; once he saw in the distance the flash of a golden star, gliding rapidly across the earth. But these animals had become, by dint of constant flight, more wary than so many antelope. Each time that he drew close, he heard the signal whinnying, faint and far; and then the herd dissolved in distance and sent back to his ears only the subdued thunder of trampling hoofs.

He was not surprised by the difficulties. He would have been amazed had they been less. And the resolution of Silvertip hardened like steel when it is properly tempered in ice water.

It was close to evening when he saw smoke rising in a thin gesture across the sky. At the base of that smoke he found two men camped in a small mesquite tangle, with a muddy blotch of a water hole near by. They gave him a wave of the hand and continued their cookery.

His gelding was thirsty enough to have drunk the filthy water as it stood, green scum and all. But Silvertip kept him back until a trench had been dug beside the water hole, a foot or so from the edge of it. Slowly that trench filled with liquid filtered through the intervening wall of sand, and out of that Silver let the weary horse drink its fill.

In the meantime, he took note that his was the first filter hole that had been dug beside the water, and that the little lump-headed mustangs of the other two men were hardly of the gear or type that would be expected to come within speaking distance of Parade. It was apparent that the two were on the trail of the great stallion; it was equally clear that they were hunting, not his body but his scalp.

With his gelding hobbled to feed on the wretched rags of grass that grew among the mesquite, Silvertip went over to the camp of the strangers.

They looked like two brothers. They kept the hair on head and face conveniently short by means of clippers that had left the marks of their cutting. They wore, also, grease-blackened canvas coats, in spite of the heat of the desert evening; and they had bright, small, squinting eyes. One of them was cleaning his rifle. Silvertip sat down cross-legged and began to eat his supper.

They could have offered him some of their food, when they saw that he was chewing parched corn only. But it was only after a long interval that one of them said:

"There's a drop of coffee here. I'll give it to you. The rest of our chuck, we're goin' to need it, maybe."

"I don't want the coffee," said Silver. "On a trail like

63

this, I want to cut right down to the essentials, for a beginning. Parched corn is good enough for me."

"Maybe a sage hen could live on that dead feed," said one of the bearded men. "It don't look human nor right nor nacheral, to me."

"It takes some chewing," said Silver. "That's all it needs."

"Look here," said the other man, "you're a long ways out to be havin' nothin' but that. You mean to say that you ain't got no bacon or salt or coffee or flour or nothin' like that along with you?"

"A man can travel a lot better light than he can loaded," answered Silver. "I'll stick to the corn till I catch my horse."

The two looked sharply at one another.

"What hoss you lost?" they asked.

"A chestnut stallion with black points," said Silvertip.

"He's lost a chestnut stallion, Chuck," said one of the men gravely.

"Yeah. With black points, Lefty," said "Chuck." He asked Silver: "You might be meanin' Parade?"

"That's the one," said Silvertip.

He looked away from the others, as though the sudden keenness of their eyes meant nothing to him. The sun was down. All the hollows were filled with blue dusk; a black mesa, rimmed with light, stood in the west, and out of the east marched purple headlands. Far above, like clouds in the sky, hung the white heads of the mountains.

"You say he's your hoss, partner?" asked "Lefty," as he paused in the cleaning of his rifle.

"He's my horse," said Silvertip.

He saw the eyes of the others glint as they exchanged glances.

"Buy him or trade for him or breed him?" asked Chuck shortly.

"I looked at him," said Silvertip, "and he's mine."

Suddenly Lefty broke into laughter.

"He looked at Parade, and Parade belongs to him," said Lefty.

"Bought him with a look," said Chuck. "Cheap at the price, eh?"

"Dirt cheap," said Lefty. "What would you do if you had him, stranger? Show him to folks at a nickel a look?"

"When I catch him up," said Silvertip, "I'll know what to do with him, all right."

"Yeah—when you catch him up," said Lefty, sneering.

Chuck pointed.

"You usin' a one-hoss outfit to catch Parade?" he asked.

"That's my outfit," said Silvertip.

The two men looked at one another and broke into fresh laughter that ended suddenly, as though they were unused to the sound and it had startled them somewhat.

"There's some," said Chuck, "that've come up here into the Sierra Blanca with twenty men and fifty hosses, all to try and catch Parade, but they ain't caught him. Maybe you'll have better luck with one hoss. Maybe brains'll make up the difference.'

"Maybe they will," said Silvertip. "All I want is a chance."

He rose, having finished the munching of that difficult meal. From the dying fire he picked out a small stick of wood, the end of which was a glowing coal. He flung it far into the air, drew a Colt, and fired. A puff of sparks flared dimly in the evening light and died out. There was no sound of the wood striking lightly on the ground, afterward. Chuck and Lefty stared at one another.

"What's the idea of that?" asked Lefty suddenly, and with a changed voice.

"I have to keep my hand in, that's all," answered Silver. "There's likely to be trouble before me."

"You goin' to crease Parade? Is that your idea?" asked Lefty.

"No," said Silvertip. "That's not the idea. But the fact is that people tell me about a parcel of skunks who are out here in the Sierra Blanca hunting for Parade, not because they ever want to sit on his back, the way I do, but because they want the thousand-dollar reward that's been put on his head."

He paused, and put up his revolver. The silence was perfect, except that the fire crackled dimly.

"If you should run into anybody of that sort," said Silvertip, "you might tell 'em that the man who shoots Parade will have to shoot me afterward. Otherwise he won't have a chance to enjoy the thousand dollars he pulls down."

"You'd go after him, eh?" said Lefty.

"The way I'd go after a mad dog," agreed Silvertip. "I'd shoot him on sight, and no jury in this neck of the woods would ever convict me for doing it. Not to the man who kills my horse."

"What I ain't quite figured," said Chuck softly, "is just how you come to own Parade."

"I'll tell you how it happened," said Silvertip. "He was made for me, and now I've come to get him. That's the reason."

CHAPTER XII

THE PURSUIT

THERE WAS NO PLAN IN THE MIND OF SILVERTIP ANY more than there is in the mind of a wolf when it settles to the long trail behind an elk, in winter; there was simply a consuming hunger that drove him on. He got sixty miles a day out of his gelding, for six days. Then he saw that the limit of endurance had been reached, and he abandoned the animal in a spot where there was both good water and good grass. The saddle had to stay behind, of course, and so did everything else of weight, except the main essentials. These were a forty-foot manila rope of the closest weave, a quantity of parched corn, a bridle, a Colt with a few rounds of ammunition.

The heavy gun would have been left behind, also, but Silver had to keep in mind the statement which he had made to Lefty and Chuck. By the grace of fortune, they might have spread the news of his threat far and wide, by this time; and in the Sierra Blanca the law is thinner than the clear mountain air. It might well be that some of the headhunters would combine to drop down upon him and wipe him out, before they went ahead with their hunting of the stallion.

Many men, of course, were crossing and recrossing the desert on the trail of the famous horse; but no one before, like Silvertip, had been mad enough to attempt the pursuit on foot.

He walked fifty miles the first day, in his narrow riding

boots. After a five-hour halt for sleep, he could not force his bleeding, swollen feet back into the boots.

He cut them up and tied the pair of leather soles under his feet, as sandals. They made wretched footgear. His feet overlapped the narrow soles; blisters began to rise. But he tramped forty miles that day, and came right up with the herd in the dusk of the evening. He was a scant hundred yards from the outskirts of the horses before the alarm sounded.

They went away like a flock of geese volleying through the air. Behind them, from the left, the golden stallion swept across the rear, brushing the stragglers before him; and to the dazed eyes of Silvertip it seemed that fire flew from the feet of the horse.

Into the gathering night they charged, and Silvertip went on, in spite of the tormenting pains of his feet. Twice more, through the dark of the night, he roused them, for they must not sleep or rest at ease. That was the main point of his plan. He had ridden far enough to wear out their first strength, but only constant nagging would suffice to reduce them to the point where he could have his chance at the golden horse.

In the dawn, he fashioned a new pair of sandals out of the tops of the boots. They were rudely made. They allowed his feet to slip and slide. Sand worked into them and cut at his skin like gnawing rodents. But he forced himself to walk on. Only by maintaining a marching gait could he ever win.

Over the horse herd he had one vast advantage—that the horses had to pause for hours every day in order to pick up enough grazing to support them while, for his own part, he could eat and still march along. And they could only carry water in their bellies, whereas he could keep the canteen at his hip well filled. But all of these advantages were wasted unless he could keep up a steady, forcing march.

He went for three days of torment, until the improvised sandals had been worn to rags. Then a coyote came imprudently near to his camp, one evening, and got a bullet between the eyes. Silver made new sandals out of part of that hide. The rest of the skin he stretched on mesquite twigs, roughly tied together to make a frame, and when he started the march this day, he carried the frame across his shoulders, so that the skin might cure in the sun. At intervals, when he paused, he rubbed the coyote's own fat and brains into the drying leather.

Baked all day, and all the next day, in the fierce sun of the Sierra Blanca, that hide had become fairly good leather before he cut from it another pair of sandals and fitted them to his battered feet.

Every step was now a torment, and still he forced himself to the swinging stride. He dreamed of shoes. Even the battered old flopping shoes of a crippled beggar would have been heaven to him. The strain told on the unsupported arch of his instep. The muscles up the shin and the back of the calf revolted against this new pressure. When he permitted himself to rest, shooting pains darted through his legs and up into his body. When he rose to walk again, he could literally hear the blood crushed out from his wounded feet.

He began to tear up his underclothing, his shirt, even his outer clothes, to make bandages.

In those few days, he had grown thin. At the end of eight days of marching, he looked at himself in the stagnant surface of a water hole and saw a starved face, lips chapped until they were white, eyes buried in shadows. His ribs stood out, and when he dropped his chin, it struck against the great bony arch of his chest. Every ounce of fat had been whipped away from him—and still his diet was parched corn, and his work was almost twenty hours a day of steady marching.

He went on. He knew, with the close of every day, that this was the end; but the next morning he was gone again on the trail, and the vision of the stallion drew him forward almost from step to step.

Results began to show now. Those fine horses from the Larchmont place, which had been so hunted before, were the first to fall to the rear. He passed them, one after another, gaunt, failing skeletons. It was a bitter temptation to put a bullet through the head of one of them and use the incalculable masses of hide to make for himself new, capacious moccasins; but he knew that such theft is worse than murder, and he had to let those beaten horses fall back past him.

Then, one day, he found himself listening to a laughing, raving voice. It was his own. The realization shocked him out of the trance into which he had walked. He found his lips twitching, his hands opening and shutting convulsively, and in his brain the streaming of a vacant wind that would contain no thought.

He needed better food than parched corn, that was clear, so he used two valuable bullets to kill two mountain grouse as he struggled through the foothills that day. He spent twenty-four hours marching slowly, pausing now and again to build a fire and roast portions of the flesh. When that food was consumed, he lay down and slept ten hours. On rising, he was a new man.

His feet now pained him less. They were scarred, deformed, swollen into horrible things; but they were not tormenting him so much. New callouses were spreading. There were few germs in this air to infect the wounds, and gradually they dried up. At every halt, he exposed them to the burning strength of the sun, and the sun itself seemed to be a miraculous healing agent.

It became less a matter of the torment in his feet than of the strength of his body. That strength never had failed him before, but it was doing so now. Still he kept the same swinging stride, no matter how his muscles yearned to shorten it.

And the horses of the herd were dropping out, day after day, day after day. The mustangs now failed continually, and he saw them fall past him to the rear, gaunt creatures, often standing with eyes closed and heads hanging, as though they had decided to wait for death to strike them down and free them from the torment of this pursuit.

But there remained, at the last, an old mare and the shining stallion. She was thin enough, and she went with a limp in one foreleg, yet she managed to keep going. As for Parade, sometimes it seemed to the bitter heart of Silvertip that he had marched all this distance in vain, seeing that the great horse appeared as rounded and smooth and filled with power as ever. Only now and then, when luck brought him quite close, could Silver discover that the stallion was stripped finer than before. The whole outline and splendor of the animal were unaltered; but when the sun fell at a certain angle, the shadows between the ribs appeared.

Sometimes, also, it appeared certain to Silvertip that, even if he came within rope-throw of the horse, he would

69

not be able to accomplish anything. Unless he managed to catch the stallion by a foot, how could Parade be thrown? Silver was no master with a rope. With knife or gun he was at home, but he had not invested many of the days of his life in the dull, honest work of a ranch.

In fact, he was not thinking a great deal of what he would do in the end. The goal that drew him was quite blind. Somehow, in some way, he would finally be able to touch the golden stallion with his hand. That was all. That was the end of his desire. After that, a miracle would give the possession of Parade to him. It was, he told himself, a sort of gigantic game of tag. When he touched Parade, the game would have ended!

There was little or no difficulty in keeping to the trail now. In the beginning, sometimes the stallion would put a great many miles, suddenly, between him and his pursuer, and on every one of those instances he would have dropped the hunter for good and all, except that the course of Parade, when he bolted away, was always straight; by an air line it could be followed. Now, a dozen times in a single day, the vision of the old mare and the shining horse would come into the eyes of Silver, but never without making his heart swell suddenly, never without lightening his step.

He had gone on for thirty days, through the burning sun of the Sierra Blanca. He was blackened to the color of a half-breed, when he came, at last, to what seemed to him the suicide of Parade.

It was a thing that he could not believe, at first. It was his understanding of the thoroughness with which Parade knew the entire Sierra Blanca that made the thing more grotesque. But the fact was that, when he followed the stallion to the mouth of Salt Creek, he saw the old mare drifting sluggishly south, away from the entrance, while the hoof marks of Parade went straight on into the mouth of the ravine.

Suicide—for a horse in the condition of Parade, it certainly seemed no less, for Salt Creek was a narrow cleft that led through the foothills, straight into the heart of the Sierra Blanca, for a hundred and twenty miles. And through the course of all those miles it was fenced on either side by time-polished cliffs, hundreds of feet high.

There are greater canyons than Salt Creek, but all have

water flowing through them, the visible agent of the visible work. Yet water was nowhere near Salt Creek. Through a hundred and twenty miles of it, the traveler could wander, the sand underfoot as white as salt, the heat confined and focused by the cliffs, the air almost always unstirred by any wind. And not until the head of the terrible valley is reached is there water.

These things must have been known to Parade, and yet he had entered the gap willingly. That was why the heart of Silver stood still, and he groaned to himself incredulously: "Suicide!"

CHAPTER XIII

SALT CREEK

TO THE STALLION, IT HAD BEEN A STRUGGLE AS BITTER, almost, as it had been to Silvertip. Parade had been hunted before, but never like this. He had been challenged by whole troops of fine horses, ridden by the craft of the Great Enemy. He had met those challenges, thrown off those troops, beaten the brains of the Enemy.

And now came this other thing that hardly seemed a danger, that seemed no more, in fact, than the shadow that trails under a cloud. It had been a mere nothing, at first. The herd had been reluctant to run from the poor creature that walked alone in pursuit of them. Only by degrees, the leader realized that the same solitary form which so often dropped beneath the horizon, was always reappearing. On the wind he had studied the scent of this man a thousand times. He had been close enough to know something of the gaunt body, too, and the tireless, swinging stride, and the ragged clothes that blew in the wind like feathers.

They had endured. The whole herd had endured, but always the strain was telling. If they ran fifty miles in a straight line, exhausting the younger and the older members of the band, nevertheless, within half a day, before the legs of the colts had well stopped shaking, the man was again in sight. At last the Great Enemy seemed personified in that terrible, lonely figure.

From Parade to the youngest colt, not one of the herd dared to drink in peace, but all lifted their heads with a jerk after a few throatfuls. None of them dared to graze with quiet minds, in spite of the sentinels which were scattered on every side to keep the lookout. It was not that they feared that the stalker could actually run up on them, but because the danger had appeared so often that it was lodged in their hearts and minds.

When the Great Enemy drew near, it was as a ghost appears to children, a thing that froze the body and the soul.

Then, after long endurance, the herd began to melt away. It was, to Parade, as the destruction of his army is to a warlike king. He had gloried in his power. He had reveled in the many heads which lifted at his call, in the bright eyes that watched him for commands, in the sleek, swift bodies that fled with him over the plains and through the valleys of the Sierra Blanca. Now they were deserting.

The better bred horses went first. Their bodies were worn; they had lost spirit; the strength went out of their resolution; they stumbled even when they went at a walk; they refused to lie down, because the alarm might come again at any moment of the night or the day.

They melted away and fell to the rear, first of all. Then the toughest of the mustangs followed, one by one, or in little groups. Surrender was in the air, except for the pair of them, Mischief and Parade himself.

As for Mischief, she had kept up to the last because her nerves had been trebly tempered by dangers of this sort long before. She could graze undisturbed until the Great Enemy was actually upon them. She could lie down to sleep by day or night, with a quiet mind. In spite of her lameness, she was ever with the leaders.

Then even Mischief began to give way. She was "tucked up." Her belly drew to a gaunt line. Her back roached up. Her head sank. Her forehoofs were beveled at the toes by constant scraping against the sand and the rocks over which she wandered. That was her condition when she and the stallion came opposite the mouth of Salt Creek, on that day.

And Parade, naturally turning away from the entrance

to that death place, was stopped by the whinny of his mother. She stood pointing her head at it and saying: "This is the way to escape!"

Parade snorted the dust from his nostrils.

"Look at the bushes at the top of the cliffs," he said. "Even the sage-brush is dying. It means two days of travel to go through that place. We tried it once, long ago. Do you remember the spring when the rains came so hard, and we went in here, thinking that there would be water everywhere? But we were wrong. There was nothing except a puddle here and there, and we were glad of the puddle water, even before we came to the water hole at the head of the valley. Now it's the middle of summer, and how could we live through it?"

The old mare sniffed at the ground, then raised her head and smelled at the air.

"He is coming," she said. "The Great Enemy has followed you week after week, but even he walks more slowly through the heat of the day. And his feet cannot move so quickly. Go through the valley of fire, my son, and when you come out on the other side, he will not be behind you. If he enters, he will die on the white sands, of thirst and the heat. You will leave him behind you, like a wolf caught in quicksands. Then we shall be free again. This is not freedom that we have now. Better to be closed into the corral of the Enemy than to have his shadow falling across your feet every day. Go quickly. I shall turn the other way. You know where we meet!"

The golden stallion turned, and he saw, rising out of a swale in the desert, the Great Enemy himself, the ragged clothes blowing in the wind like many tattered flags. Certainly it was better to pass through the fire than to let this creature like a leech cling to the trail. So he gave to Mischief a farewell whinny, and jogged straight forward into the jaws of the valley of death.

His was no longer the light, swinging trot that sprang across easy going or hard with such infinite ease. Instead, his hoofs trailed, and his hind legs seemed to be sinking away from beneath the burden they had to bear.

Presently, as the sand grew deep, he fell back to a walk. The heat rose like fire from the white surface of the sand, and like walls of flame it burned along the polished faces of the cliffs on either side.

Sweat rolled out on his hide and dripped from his belly. Not a breath of air came to cool him, only stirrings of warmer and warmer currents, like the ripplings of hot water in a pot. Where the sand rose above his hoofs, it burned him to the fetlock joints, and higher still.

It wound like a snake through most of its course, this valley of despair, and, coming out into a straighter part of the passage, he looked back and saw that the Great Enemy had indeed come into the trap. Exultation filled Parade. He arched his proud neck again and sent down the valley a neigh that was a challenge indeed.

So it was accepted by the man.

"He thinks I'm beaten," said Silvertip to himself. "And maybe I am. I don't know. Maybe I am!"

He freshened his pace. The muscles across his stomach began to ache. He bent his body a little to favor them. His legs were numb. Breathing was difficult. And always in the looseness of the sand his feet kept slipping back.

The stallion broke into a trot that carried him swiftly out of sight around the next bend.

When Silvertip came to that corner in turn, he could look more than half a mile straight ahead—and Parade was not in view!

Then Silvertip got to the shadow of a rock that had fallen from the edge of the cliff above him, and he slumped down where his head and his half-naked body would be protected from the sun.

The arm on which he leaned shuddered with weakness. Dizziness kept his brain turning, for it seemed almost hotter in the shadow than it had been in the full blaze of the light.

He took off his sandals and looked at his battered feet. His right foot was twitching with every pulse of his blood, and the red stain was continually growing from some new wound, or from an old one that had recently been chafed open.

He told himself that he was beaten. The neigh of the stallion still grew up in his mind and echoed freshly. He was beaten. He was trapped. What lay before him he could not tell, but he knew that it was more than twelve miles to pass on the rear trail to get to water. Twelve miles—and a pint of water to get him there!

He took his canteen from his hip and swirled the water

in it. It was a liquid that had now arrived at almost blood temperature. But it was moisture, and moisture he must have.

He looked down at his hand, and it seemed the hand of an old man, trembling as with an ague, so great was his weakness. If his hand shook like this, of what use could a heavy revolver and bullets be to him?

He took out the Colt, aimed at a near-by rock, and fired. The bullet missed! He tried again, steadying the weapon with both hands, but again the shaking of his muscles made the shot fail.

Suddenly he hurled the gun from him, and caught out the extra ammunition and threw it after the gun. Every ounce of extra burden that he carried was an ounce of life-blood drawn from his heart.

He stood up, and the blaze of the sunshine covered him as with fire. That blasting heat scorched him through and through. It cast a fume up his nostrils; all the landscape wavered before his eyes.

It was only common sense, not weakness, that determined him to turn back to cover the known twelve miles to the water hole. He would only go forward to the end of this straight stretch, and from the next corner try to take his farewell glimpse of Parade.

So he went on to the next bend, and, looking down the exposed ravine for more than a mile, he found no trace of the stallion—there was only the trail that went straight ahead, and vanished. Now, those hoof marks were not entirely straight, but here and there they meandered, as the sign of Parade never had wavered before, in all the miles he had followed the horse.

This gave him the flickering gleam of a new hope. It was the way of Parade to move as straight as a bird through the air; and if he were faltering now, might he not be near to dropping out of the fight?

The thought made the big man forget all his troubles, the heat of the sun, the anguish of his feet. If the great horse were near to failing, he, Silvertip, would be on hand to see the last moment. He would strive to get there at least in time to see the last light of life in those wild eyes.

So Silvertip found himself stumbling vaguely, feebly

forward and continually straightening his leaning body to save himself from pitching down on his face.

After that, the best of his senses left him. He walked on. All he knew was that he was continually walking. He could hardly tell in which direction he was going, but he was walking on and on.

Once he came to himself with a hand of fire laid across his face, and he found that he was staggering, his head swayed far back on his shoulders. He was frightened. He dropped on one knee and put the knuckles of his hand on the burning sands.

"I'm going out on my feet," said Silvertip to himself. "I've got to do something about it."

And then, with laughter that cracked his lips, he remembered that he actually was carrying water with him! The canteen had gone out of his crazed mind.

He took a tablespoonful to moisten his mouth. He took more, and more, in swallows so small that they would hardly have sufficed for a bird. But he knew that this was the proper economy. Small drinks, and many of them.

The sun dropped. He dropped with it, flat on his back, and watched the angry fires climb the sky, and wane again toward darkness. But the heat still radiating from the ground scorched him and made his head ache.

He sat up, stripped off his rags, put them on the warm sand, and stretched out on this bed, naked. Then he went to sleep.

He dreamed that he had fallen into a river of ice; he wakened to find that the heat of the day was gone, and in its place a wind off the mountain snows was cutting through the ravine. His body was congealed to pale iron, so he dressed, and went on.

The pain in his feet shut out all other thoughts presently. He could forget the cold, because of that greater agony. And now the cold was gone, and the pain from the feet was gone, also, since the aching of his entire body recommenced. It was strange that mere walking should be an act that required such an effort of the volition. He began to swing his arms, so that the forward momentum of his entire body would be increased, and in this way he strode on, until he was stepping out at the ordinary pace to which he had forced himself all through the hunt. Once that pace was established, it maintained itself, as it were.

He rounded a corner. Something dark struggled a moment against the pale starlight on the sand; then the figure of a horse lurched to its feet not ten yards aways, and went cantering down the valley, each stride longer than the one preceding.

It was Parade, and not until the horse was out of sight did Silvertip realize that he had been near enough to make the cast with his rope, and try to end this frightful chase!

CHAPTER XIV

THE POOL

THE DARKNESS THICKENED, AT LAST. NO, IT WAS ONLY that the mountains in the distance and the rock walls of the valley appeared to be growing more black. Something in his memory recognized that effect and connected it with a dim hope, a thing of pleasure. And after a moment he realized that the dawn was beginning.

Looking up, he was like one sunk in water, staring through the thick film of the sea toward mountain heights that now loomed closer. At first, the fire of the day seized on the snows, then glinted on the stone flanks of the mountains, and finally slid down into the hollow of Salt Creek itself.

He knew that he was exhausted, but he knew that he dared not halt; that he must use the blessed coolness of these early hours, while he could still keep his legs swinging in rhythm. Thirst was no longer a part of heat; it was a part of cold, and seemed to help the ice of the air to pass through him.

But it was not long until a blaze of pale light flared in the east, so brightly that he had to blink his eyes a little. And a little later the sun was looking down at him. The very first stroke of it went to his heart, like a touch of fever. His knees shook. He had endured much during the day before, but he knew that he could not pass through this day.

Out of that certainty, he told himself that he would

simply go on until he could go no longer, and then find a place among the shadows where he might lie down and die. And so it was that, making a turn of the sinuous valley, he came upon view of Parade.

But he was on parade no longer. That glorious head was sunk at last. The shimmering tail hung straight down, the hocks knocking it back and forth at every step. The head of the stallion bobbed with each stride, and about his hoofs, never lifted clear, the sand was swishing. Silver heard the sound of it, like water, and he shouted, waving his arms wildly, running forward.

The stallion lurched into a trot, with labor, like an old plow horse. Finally, with a supreme effort, Parade swung into his gallop. It was a mere caricature of his usual wind-free gait, but a gallop it was that drifted the horse swiftly away from the pursuer. As Parade strained forward, the pulling muscles of his flanks, and his laboring lungs, made the bones of his ribs thrust out. His hips were two up-thrusting elbows. His withers were a great lump. His back sagged. The velvet and the sheen were both gone from his starving coat.

"He's dying," said Silver to himself. "He's dying, and I'm dying on my feet, too. But, before I die, I'm going to have my rope around his neck!"

He took another swallow of the water. There was less than a cupful remaining, and the sound of it swishing lightly in the canteen was death music to Silvertip.

A queer sense of doom came over him—that he would not be permitted to die until he had placed his hand upon the body of the horse. Therefore, he strode on and on. The fear was gone from him. It was not hope of life that sustained him, but that other strange hope.

He came in sight of the stallion again. The horse had halted, head down once more, feet braced. This time, thought Silver, he would surely be able to put the rope on the tall skeleton.

But he was wrong. At his nearer approach, Parade was able to lift himself into a trot, and then to a reeling gallop.

Sudden pity struck through the heart of the man as he saw that unhappy sight, but the pity was crushed by the sterner emotion. If they were found dead, the two of them, it would be with his rope around the neck of Parade, and the end of that rope tied to his hand, in sure

78

sign that he had conquered the stallion before death destroyed them both.

That would be something of a monument to leave behind him. Enough people had come into the Sierra Blanca with their outfits of men and horses to appreciate the supreme thing that he would have accomplished.

The heat of the day grew. Long before noon, delirium attacked his mind, and he was never in his right senses for more than an hour at a time during the rest of that day. In that madness of the mind, sometimes it seemed to him that the horse which staggered before him was not a skeleton, but the full beauty, the full power of the great Parade. And he himself was pursuing the speeding monster on wings.

He could not know that they were involuntarily trying to save one another—that the stallion did not lie down to die merely because the man pursued him, and that Silver himself did not drop because the haunting vision of the horse was continually in the corner of his eye.

Twice that day, he tried the rope. Once he missed completely. Once the loop slapped on the hip of the horse, and sent Parade off at a blundering, swaying trot. Galloping was now impossible, and even a trot could not be sustained for more than fifty yards at a time.

If bitter compassion at times poured through Silvertip, thinking of the wreck of the beauty of the horse, he looked down at his own skeleton body, and set his teeth again.

A sane man would have doubted his senses, if he had observed that picture. But there was no sanity save the lust for power in Silvertip now, and in the horse there was a fear of the Great Enemy, greater than the fear of death.

More than their bodies could accomplish, they now performed. The day went on, bitterly, slowly, hour by hour, until the sun had gone well beyond the zenith. Then the stallion halted, and, for all his desire to close in, Silvertip had to slump down in the shade of a rock.

There he gathered his strength, bit by bit, summoning his force, breathing deep, snorting like an animal to clear his nostrils of dust.

At last he could rise and go on with shaking legs; but, as he came near, again Parade went lumbering forward.

And the fiercest heat of the day began, burning them, scalding them both. The canteen had long been empty, and for two days the stallion had gone through that oven without water.

The afternoon wore through. The blaze of the sun was less terrific, but the contained heat of the valley seemed thicker and deeper than ever. There was no oxygen in the air, and the mouth of Silvertip opened wide, though he knew that it was fatal to breathe that dusty atmosphere through the mouth for any length of time.

And then, in the twilight, he saw far before them a beautiful mirage of a blue pool, with two trees standing beside it, and a green fringe of grass.

If it were a mirage, it was strange that the stallion should drag himself toward it at a lumbering trot. If it were a mirage, it was stranger still that the birds should dip out of the sky to cut the surface with their beaks.

It was no mirage at all, he realized with a sudden wildness of joy. It was water, beyond doubt. It was honest water, which God had placed there at the end of the trail for the suffering.

Silvertip on staggering knees, began to run in turn. His legs turned to quicksilver. He fell on his face, rolled, crawled forward on his knees and on his hands, with his elbows bending beneath his weight, until his fingers were in the wet margin of the pool.

Already the stallion had thrust his muzzle into the surface, sending small waves across the water, and Silvertip, stretched out on his gaunt stomach, drank like an animal, and lifted his head to breathe, and drank again.

By a greater miracle than the actual presence of the water, it was cool. Silver thrust his arms into it, and it rippled over his flesh like a blessing over the soul of the damned. He laughed, and strangled, and drank again and again.

Then he pushed himself back, and saw the stallion on the farther side of the water, watching him with red eyes. Knee-deep stood Parade, and the dust was washed from his face almost to the eyes, he had plunged in his head so deeply.

Silvertip coiled his rope.

The stallion flinched—then he lowered his head to drink again, blinking as he did so.

Now Silvertip stood erect, the noose ready, strength rapidly beginning in his body, the certainty of victory in his soul. He swung the rope—and still the horse drank, with the shadow flying in circles across that very mirror into which he had dipped his head.

The hand of Silvertip dropped. The rope struck lightly against the green of the grass.

For suddenly it had seemed to him that this was a sacred spot, removed from the strifes of the world and hallowed by some more-than-mortal law.

He stared at Parade, and saw the great horse in the hollow of his hand, yet he could not throw the noose. It was not water that he had drunk; it was not water that the horse was still drinking; it was life.

Silvertip looked up with a groan to the darkening twilight in the sky, and when he glanced down again, Parade was drawing back from the verge of the pool, drawing back from the range of the rope, moving again into a world of freedom. And still Silvertip stood entranced, and could not lift his hand.

CHAPTER XV

THE NEW WORLD

PARADE, WITHDREW FROM THE REACH OF THE ROPE, blundered only a few steps before he lay down beneath a tree. He saw the man come a few uncertain, wavering steps after him, then sink to the ground in turn. The thicker night, more perfect in silence, drew over them, with stars in the heaven above them, and more brightly in the water at their side.

Still the two rested, motionless, like two heroes of some legendary combat who have battled together from dawn to midday, and in the heat withdraw from one another a little and lie down to rest, by mutual consent, well knowing that they will soon rise again and join the struggle once more.

The man lay on his face, his head pillowed in his arms. Parade could see that, and something out of the human face spoke to him continually through the dark of the night. Eyes were on Parade, passing through his body, it seemed, and finding the spirit within. He could not believe that he was actually lying there, prone and passive, while the Great Enemy, personified in one man, lay near by, a danger ready to spring. Yet the agony of weariness controlled him. The eyes of Parade closed, and his mind wandered in sleep, constantly broken as his eyes winked open again and again.

He heard a sound of regular, loud breathing from the Great Enemy. Sometimes it seemed to him that the man was gathering, and rising to his feet; and again, as he jerked his own head high, it seemed to Parade that the Great Enemy was merely sleeping.

There was enough of the savage beast in Parade to make him think of lurching to his feet and charging that frail body. One stroke of a forehoof should be enough to shatter the life in it. And there was not the formidable scent of iron and gunpowder, warning him away. But Mischief had always declared that there is in man a mystery of power, incomprehensible and vast, so that, for all his fragility, the Great Enemy is always dangerous. Moreover, in the heart of Parade there was welling a strange sense of fear, and something that was different from fear.

It was like that emotion which comes between day and night, or between night and morning; it was like standing on a high hill and looking at a new country. There was the sense of something infinite, and infinitely worth exploring.

The hours went by like a swift river. The mountains began to darken in the east, and Parade knew that the day was coming. He got to his feet, with an effort. There was no returning down the length of Salt Creek, he knew, because of the fluid weakness which coursed through him. One more day without water would be the end of him, in his condition. There remained only one way, and that was ahead, up the trail that wound dimly into the higher mountains; for he was now at the very head of Salt Creek.

Would the man rise, also?

Yes, Parade had hardly made three steps when Silvertip stirred, groaned, and then rose to his feet, and stood swaying.

He drank from the pool again, put something from a

pocket into his mouth, and stepped out limping on the trail of the stallion. It seemed to Parade that it would always be like this—that, as he struggled through the world, this two legged creature would follow him, with the snaky rope in his hand.

More hope came to the horse when he found that he had regained some of his lost strength after water and rest. He struck forward at a trot. The ground lifted. He wound rapidly up and up through a maze of rocks. Before him, above him, the sun struck on polished boulders never been able to accomplish what this Great Enemy had and flamed on the blue-white ice of the summits, half lost in the sky.

There was another land beyond those peaks, and Mischief had told him of it. The passes were narrow and dangerous, but if he could get through them, he would come out into a green world, and his strength would soon return to him and his limbs be robed with power, as before. All of those men who had striven to catch him had done—drive him at last out of the hot fastnesses of the Sierra Blanca.

As he climbed, he had many a glimpse behind and beneath him of the lower country. He could see the whole course of Salt Creek winding away toward the open desert. Through that crystal morning he could make out small forms; and, in a valley close to Salt Creek, two horsemen were striking in toward the mountains.

Well for Parade that he had met no horsemen during these last terrible days! They could have run him down in a moment, and ensnared him with their ropes.

He seemed to have climbed, now, into the heart of the dawn itself, and the morning light was seeping down from the higher levels over a darker earth beneath. Then the sun itself poured over him like a warm liquid.

He stood out on a projecting point, for an instant. It was like the prow of a ship, and he, as the lookout, stared far away through the sea of mountains. He had risen, now, to the level of the snow. A gray bank of it lay along the ledge, at one side. Beneath the stunted pines there were bits and sparklings of it. It was the first promise of the region of wind and ice that lay above him.

Then the Great Enemy came up around the bend below. He had a stick in his hand, and leaned some of his weight on it. He climbed stolidly, with slow steps, his head swaying a little from side to side. A sort of angry despair came over the stallion, made him toss up his head, and brought a trumpet-sounding neigh from his throat. The violence of his call made his knees tremble. But the man did not even look up. He came on, slowly, steadily, step after step, as remorseless as time.

Parade turned and fled as fast as he could up the next rise. He looked back. The rocks had blotted out the form of the man, but, of course, he would be coming. Like a wolf, he seemed to have a nose that told him the way, and the fear of the stallion grew into a blind panic that scourged him wildly forward.

He gained a height. He fled down a steep-sided hollow. He rushed the rising ground beyond, and found himself trembling and already exhausted on the bitter upward slope that seemed to have no ending. Far beneath him, he saw the man coming, plodding with the stick, head down, swaying slightly from side to side!

There was no wind on these heights, though usually the storms must have flowed like invisible rivers, to judge from the manner in which trees were blown back at timber line. And immediately above was the white world of the snow. Later in the year it would shrink upward and upward, until there were glistening caps on only a few of the loftiest peaks, but now the mountains were drowned in it, and the passes choked. A crunching and squeaking sound kept coming from the pressure of his hoofs on the snow crystals.

It was slow going. There were few levels; it was always up and down, with need to step like a cat for fear a false step on the treacherous snow would hurl him over the lip of some vast canyon.

It was a new world. A mountain sheep, almost as big as a pony, ran across the path of the stallion and hurled itself over the edge of a cliff—to be dashed to pieces beneath, it seemed! But no, it was caroming from side to side of a narrow crevice, seeming to strike on its head at the bottom of every jump, rebounding sidewise and ever downward like a great rubber ball.

The horse, eying that descent, felt suddenly weak and helpless. Then the snow before him became alive, and white ptarmigans rose on purring wings and shot away in a long, low flight, arrowy fast.

All creatures here were new, and their newness brought home to the stallion a sense of doom. To be in such a fantastic world was almost like being dead.

And the man? He was still coming. Step after step, at the unvarying rhythm, he climbed the steep way, and the footmarks which he left behind were spots of his own crimson blood. The stippled trail moved far away behind him before it dipped out of sight. The wind blew softly from that direction, and the stallion distinctly smelled the freshness of new blood.

Another panic overcame him, at that. Slipping, sliding, groaning with fear, he rushed along the narrow trail, regardless of the thousand-foot gulf at his left, and so came out on a small platform of rock, slicked over with an incrustation of ice. Here all progress stopped. At the right, the cliff went upward at the pitch of a rising heron. At the left was the gulf. And across the ledge on which the horse had been traveling had spilled a mass of snow, mixed with ponderous boulders of ice. The sun shone full on this trap, dazzling the eyes of Parade.

He turned. He knew that the time for the final battle had come, and already he was eying the gorge at his side. Better to die there, he felt, than to pass into the mysterious hands of the enslaver, Man. He imagined the outward spring, the downward rush, the cold sweeping of wind against his belly. Perhaps he would begin to turn over and over, like a great stone. Then one last crushing blow, and life would be over.

Around the corner of the icy rock stepped the Great Enemy, and confronted him, leaning on the staff. Parade lifted his head, and sent a great neigh, a death cry, ringing through the echoing mountains. Far below, across the canyon, and on a different trail, two riders with clipped hair and close-clipped beards heard the call, and looking up, saw, in part, what happened.

CHAPTER XVI

THE CAPTURE

The snaky shadow of the rope was deploying in the hand of the Great Enemy. It slid out through the air, and hovered an instant. The stallion, trying to dodge, almost shot his weight off the slippery rock and into the abyss. As Parade regained his feet, he felt the noose whip home with a burning touch about his neck. It closed up on his windpipe. It was a cruel hand that relentlessly throttled him.

There was no chance for flight, or for pulling free. Parade did the next possible thing—he charged straight home!

Before him, he saw the man shrink aside, and the way of escape opened. Then the burly wooden staff whirled, a blur of speed before the eyes of Parade.

The blow took him between the ears and knocked him to his knees. He was at the very feet of the Great Enemy. The smell of the blood from them was a stench in his nostrils; the scent of the body of the man was terribly near; and, above all, the voice of man was ringing out at his ears, in savage victory.

Parade shrank back as he came to his knees. A loop of the rope whipped under a forefoot. He barely managed to disengage the hoof before it was jerked up toward his throat.

Again the two faced one another. Laughter came out of the throat of Man, laughter, detestable to all animals, because it is a sound which otherwise has no existence in nature. The whole mind and difference of man is expressed in that half-gasping and half-singing noise.

And seeing the Great Enemy shaken for the moment, Parade charged again. He came with teeth bared, ears flattened, his head thrust out like the head of a snake. The club whirled up. He dodged. Instantly his feet shot out from beneath him. His whole body skidded over the ice-polished rock. Beneath him was the dreadful, empty glimpse of the chasm, the white dance of water that foamed through the bottom of the ravine.

With his forehoofs, as a cat with paw and claw, the stallion clung to the verge of the cliff. His hind legs, reaching frantically upward, struck at the massed ice that underlay the ledge and knocked it away in great chunks. Then his forehoofs began to slide slowly outward.

He stopped struggling. The shuddering cold of death was already in him. And then Man leaned above him, reaching far down. The smell of blood was ranker than ever in the nostrils of Parade. The ragged clothes of the Great Enemy brushed his face, and the dust of Salt Creek filled the nostrils of the horse. It would be easy, now, to seize one of those fragile hands and crush the bone in his teeth—but miracles were happening!

Of all the mysteries of man, his hands are the most wonderful. It is they which work with fire; it is they which use iron and gunpowder; but now the hands of the Great Enemy had laid mighty hold upon the noose that encircled the neck of Parade.

Man was lifting with a power incredible in so small a thing. Man was swaying back, every instant in danger of losing his foothold and slipping out into the void. Man was pulling with such a force that the forehoofs of the horse no longer slipped outward, but worked in to gain a better grip.

The rear hoofs struck up to gain some purchase on the under ice, below the ledge. Again those striking feet merely managed to knock away great lumps. Utter despair came upon Parade. Not even the miraculous hands of Man could save him.

But Man still struggled. It was plain that the Great Enemy was risking life to save life. And how could that be true? Yet he remained there on the brink of death for them both, tugging, straining; and out of the throat of Man came new sounds, never heard before.

Man is a whooping, yelling monster. He rides horses at frantic speed, goring their flanks with terrible spurs. Man yells, in a voice that strikes through the mind like a stone through thin ice. But this time Man was speaking in a tone of sympathy and encouragement as plainly decipherable as ever was the soft whinny of a mare to its foal.

Groaningly the words came out, forced and strained by the physical effort that accompanied them.

New strength came into Parade; despair left him. With head and forelegs he pressed down on the rock; his struggling hind legs beat upward until one of them found an instant's lodgment.

That instant was enough. The pull of the man was greater than ever. Parade swayed upward; his whole body trembled for an instant in the crisis of the strain; then he lurched forward onto the safety of the little platform.

The man staggered back before him, without ever letting go the rope which encircled the throat of Parade. And the face of Man was horrible. Out of his distended jaws came the hoarse, panting breath of exhaustion. His breast heaved in and out against the very muzzle of Parade. His eyes glared, bloodstained as those of a beast of prey. His whole body swayed with weakness, and the magic hands which had saved the stallion now quivered as they retained their grasp on the noose.

There was an equal weakness in Parade. Only the wide bracing of his legs sustained him, for the time being. Then, gradually, power returned. Out of the haze of exhaustion he recovered, to realize more fully how he was bound to the man.

What he had felt the night before returned to him. He had then been on the verge, as it were, of a vast, undiscovered country, and now he felt that he was in the midst of it. The mere crossing of mountains could not be to him what this moment with the Great Enemy had meant.

He had been struck to his knees—such was the force of the magic of this puny creature—and then he had been drawn from the brink of death.

Now the hands of Man left the rope and passed upward along the soft under parts of his throat, and came over the tense muscles of the jaw, and moved with infinite delicacy across the face of Parade.

He stood entranced, for electric happiness flowed out of that touch, and the voice of Man, recommencing, made through the soul of the stallion such echoes as sing and murmur quietly down the ravine of a small mountain brook.

Danger, and starvation, and long labor, and the torments of heat and cold were forgotten; but fear, most of all, was the ghost that disappeared in this new sunshine of understanding. Years of quiet living cannot reveal our friends to us as can the cruel light of one moment of danger and need. Then the many fail, and the one is found, and to have such a one is better than all the throngs. There is no bitterness like full knowledge, and there is no such glorious happiness. And one friend is the bread of life, if his friendship has been proved.

The wisdom of the old mare, his mother, had been to the stallion a profound thing. Suddenly it shrank. It became obscure and worthless, compared with this new knowledge.

The hand of Man was laid across his forehead, then both hands blinded his eyes. But he stood without a jerk of the head, without a tremor of the body. Into the darkness of that moment, Parade was pouring his faith and his trust that no harm would come.

He heard joy come bubbling like spring water out of the throat of Man, and the flow of it invaded his own being. The hands were removed. He looked with his unblinded eyes, curiously, with only a faint comprehension, into the face of Man. And the dead centuries worked in the blood of Parade, surely—all the generations through which his race had served Man, the master, and had known Man, the friend.

The Great Enemy drew back, and pulled gently at the rope. Parade drew back against the weight. And Man stood beside him, now, softly pressing forward on the noose until Parade yielded to the pressure.

There was no harm in that. There was no harm, surely, in walking with his head at the shoulder of Man, while the voice made music in his ears.

Mischief had said that in time even some of the sounds of the voice of Man can take on a definite meaning. Parade wondered if that time would ever come for him. Even as it was, the speech had a meaning of contentment.

They went on slowly down the icy way. Parade slipped. The hand of Man, strongly sustaining, steadied him again. A little later, Man slipped in turn, and the full weight of his body dragged down against the rope until he was in balance once more.

The ears of Parade pricked forward. He was walking,

not on rock and snow and ice, but into a country of the spirit, where every step was a marvel beyond calculation.

They wound down out of the region of white snow. They passed the distorted willows and aspens of the timber line that stretched like a dark water mark, level and straight, along the sides of the mountains. They came to the kinder going beneath, and where a small dale opened, there the Great Enemy made a pause.

Deep, rich grass grew here, but Parade was regardless of it, watching the face of Man as a child watches the face of a summer sky. And Man plucked a handful of the grass, and offered it at the lips of Parade. Curiously he sniffed at it. The taint of the flesh of Man was on it, yet he gathered a little under his prehensile upper lip. The taste was not spoiled. He ate, suddenly, with eagerness. Again and again that hand was filled, and again and again Parade took the grass from it. Then handfuls of seeded grass, carefully chosen; richer food than ever Parade had been able to sort for himself.

They remained there for more than an hour, and during that hour, the voice of Man would speak, and then the silence of the wilderness would flow gently in upon them, and unutterable peace began to steal like happy sleep over the stallion.

Far away, he saw two riders moving. But what of that? He would have fled, if he had been alone, but now he was with a mighty companion, stronger than all other men, more patient than time, more enduring than heat or cold. If other men came, they were his lesser fellows, like colts in a herd to the great wild stallion that rules it.

Presently, the riders were no longer in view, but two men on foot moved carefully among the rocks and shrubbery, obviously stalking, and coming straight in the direction of Man, the Great Enemy!

This was strange! But all-knowing Man would surely know this.

Perhaps it was a game, as when colts play together in the happy summer of the year.

Then one man was kneeling, and the long line of light that ran down the barrel of a rifle narrowed and shortened to a single winking eye of light.

Well did the stallion know guns, and now he started

violently, throwing up his head, staring in the direction of that new danger.

Man arose, also, and turned, and as he turned, an audible blow struck his head and knocked him flat on his back. A thin mist had appeared around the mouth of the rifle, and now the report clanged softly against the ears of the stallion, coming vaguely through the thin mountain air.

Parade looked down. Red covered the head, red streaked the face of Man. He lay with his arms outstretched, and his eyes partially open, and a smile was on his lips. The hot, thick, sweet scent of blood filled the nostrils of Parade.

He stared toward the place from which the shot had been fired, but now there was nothing to be seen of the two men.

Parade lowered his head, and sniffed at the face of the fallen man. There was no response. He stamped. It brought no answer, though sand flew from the stamping of the hoof into the face of the Great Enemy.

A moment later, a shadow crossed near by. Parade, tossing up his head, was in time to see one of the strangers snatch up the end of the fallen rope and snub it around the point of a boulder. And Parade himself, rushing off at a gallop, came to the end of that line only to be flung heavily on his side.

He lay senseless for a moment. Meantime, both of the men were leaning over Silvertip.

"You got him, Chuck," said one of them. "You got him good, too. Right through the bean, old son."

"He's goin' to bump off the gent that takes the scalp of Parade," answered Chuck. "But he won't be doin' no bumpin' no more. Get your rope on that hoss, Lefty. He's goin' to raise the devil when he gets to his feet again. Shall we roll Silvertip down into the ravine?"

"Leave him be," answered Lefty. "The buzzards'll spoil his looks so's nobody would know him. In half a day, they'll spoil him."

CHAPTER XVII

AT PARMALEE

THEY TOOK THE STALLION ON TWO LARIATS AND HALF LED, and half dragged him away, looking back a few times, contentedly, on the body they left behind them. It was not until they were out of sight that Silvertip's head turned slightly to the side, and a groan came through his parched lips.

If they had heard it, they would have come back like tigers to finish their work, or else they would have loosed the stallion and fled away like carrion crows to a distant region. They would have separated, changed their names, shaved their faces, and striven in a new life more completely to bury themselves from the eye of Silvertip. But they went on in happy ignorance that the rifle bullet had glanced on the skull of Silver, instead of boring its way straight through the brain.

They had Parade delivered into their hands in exactly the state in which they could work on him. Half dead with fatigue, more than half starved, he looked more like an ancient caricature than the king of the Sierra Blanca desert. So one of them hauled at him from in front, and the other fed a quirt into him to urge him across the desert. He tried more than once to fight back. His spirit was not dead, but his body failed him.

When they came in sight of Mischief, hardly in better shape than her son, in spite of the fact that she had not made the frightful journey through Salt Creek, it was easy for Chuck to catch the mare, while Lefty held the stallion.

At this stroke, they exulted beyond words. They were bringing in both the stallion and the mare, where the ablest men in the West had failed. Perhaps it was true that more than a hundred thousand dollars had been spent in time, horseflesh, and other ways, in order to capture Parade. All of that money had been spent in vain. And now they were bringing him in!

There was reputation in it, in the first place. There was enough reputation to last a dozen men the course of their lives.

There was money in it, too, for what would not some rancher pay to get hold of this famous animal in order to improve his saddle stock? Besides, Parade could be showed at a quarter a head, and people would throng to see him, close at hand. His very picture would have a good cash value.

Lefty and Chuck were thrifty souls, and they talked over these prospects with a calm determination to miss no tricks. Even Mischief was of value, as the companion who for so long had gone limping at the side of Parade. She was the stamp and seal of his identity.

"It ain't what you do," said Chuck. "It's the way you do it, that counts. There's poor old Silvertip now. There's a gent that's been talked about and wrote about and sung about. And he takes and burns himself up, and he does what nobody else can do, and he gets as thin as a crow, flyin' after Parade. And what does he get out of it?"

"He gets a bullet through the head," said Lefty, grinning. "And we get Parade."

"It ain't what you do," Chuck repeated. "It's the way you do it that counts. And we've done this the right way. If that Parade don't fall down flat before we get him to a corral and some good grass."

"There ain't any hurry about that," said Lefty. "We got him weakened and we're goin' to keep him weakened till he's broke."

In this there was the sort of sense that could not fail to appeal to such a mind as that of Chuck. That same day, they put a saddle on the back of the exhausted stallion, and Lefty mounted.

There was one minute of violent bucking, one flash in the pan, one faint suggestion of the explosion that would have taken place had Parade possessed his strength, and then the big horse crumpled to the ground.

For a time they feared that he was about to die. But his body was not dead. It had been toughened through too many years of famine and pursuit to give way so suddenly now. He was able to rise again, and stumble on. And when they came to grass and water, the men spent two whole days letting the stallion and the mare recuperate.

In the olden time, Parade would have recovered with amazing speed. But now his progress was very slow. His body was still intact, but the heart and the pride in him had been almost fatally wounded.

It hardly mattered that the saddle was placed on him every day. It hardly mattered that his flanks felt the goring stroke of the spurs, or that the quirt bit into his hide, or that his tender mouth was sawed by the savage grip of the Spanish bit. The chief indignity already had befallen him. He had been mastered!

And every inch of the Sierra Blanca was an insult and a reproach to him. The ragged summits of the mountains that he had viewed so many times with a feeling of kinship and companionship, now seemed to stare down at him with scornful eyes. Behind him followed the ghosts of the fine horses which had been at his command. They were gone with his freedom, and there was no heart left in him.

Vainly Lefty and Chuck waited for a return of his magnificence, as they drifted him slowly south. Flesh appeared once more over his ribs. He was as he had been before, but the horse which responded to whip and spur was far other than the old king of the Sierra Blanca. The spring was gone from his step, the arch from his neck, the fire from his eyes. Weariness was always in him, the weariness of the spirit.

That was how they brought him into Parmalee.

The great Parmalee rodeo was about to commence; in ten days it would start, and in the meantime, visitors, cattle buyers, cowpunchers, were beginning to pour into town. It was a perfect opportunity for the showing of the stallion, and Lefty and Chuck made the most of it.

Harry Richmond had his stallion, Brandy, in a corral near the race track. Adjoining it was a high-walled inclosure used sometimes for the breaking of very refractory mustangs, with a snubbing post in the center. Here the mare and the great Parade were placed. It was a simple matter to hang cheap canvas around the inclosure so that people could not peek in. It was equally simple to build a little platform against the side of the fence, and there, for twenty-five cents, a man could stand as long as he wished to stare at the famous outlaw.

Dave Larchmont came and stood there almost half a day, with that poor Englishman, Hammersley, beside him. Hammersley was almost ruined now, men said. He carried his head as high as ever, and his back as straight, and his mustache bristled as fiercely, and his eye was as stern as when he had spent thousands upon thousands in the pursuit of Parade. But it was said that his fortune had melted away. He had spent too much time horse hunting, and not enough in the management of his place.

There was a long silence between him and Larchmont, and then Hammersley said:

"D'you know what it's really like, Larchmont?"

"It's like seeing a ghost," said Larchmont.

"No," said Hammersley, "it's like seeing the poor relation of a great man. The name may be the same, and the face may be the same, but the great heart's gone, Larchmont. The heart's gone, and nothing will bring it back again!"

Even to see the ghost, the fading relic of what Parade had once been, people were willing to come, not once, but many times. It was a poor day when Chuck and Lefty did not haul in from twenty to thirty dollars, and this was money so sweet and so easily come by that Chuck took a bit to drink, and Lefty to poker. They managed to spend their winnings in that way, easily enough.

"Suppose that Silvertip could see us now," said Chuck, one evening, as he leaned against a bar beside his partner. "He'd doggone nigh rise out of his grave, wouldn't he, Lefty?"

"Him?" snapped Lefty. "I kind of half wish that we'd left him alone."

"Whatcha talkin' about?" demanded Chuck. "Ain't it the best day's work that we ever done in our lives? Or you got an idea that murder will out, eh?"

Lefty pointed before him, at the mirror, and seemed to be squinting at his own image in the glass.

"We went and murdered Parade," he said. His face puckered.

"What kind of fool talk is this here?" demanded Chuck.

"You wouldn't understand," answered Lefty. "I was just thinkin'."

"Quit your crabbin' while the coin is rollin' in," said Chuck.

"What I mean to say," remarked Lefty, "that hoss was plumb satisfied with Silvertip. Account of bein' hauled back up over the edge of the cliff, maybe. I thought that fool of a Silver was goin' to slip over the edge himself, for a while." He shook his head.

"Are you tryin' to get mysterious, or something like that?" demanded Chuck. "Whatcha mean—the hoss bein' plumb satisfied with Silver? Didn't Silver wear Parade down? Didn't Silver nigh onto kill the both of them, he chased that hoss so long?"

"You seen Parade eatin' out of Silver's hand," said Lefty gloomily.

"Well, he'll eat out of our hands, too," said Chuck, with a grin.

"He won't," said Lefty. "I been and tried him, and he won't. You'd think that there was poison in my hand. If I take and stir up the barley or the oats for him in his feed box, he'll smell at it, but he won't eat. You try the same thing, and see."

"I've tried it—and he won't eat what I've touched," agreed Chuck. "What's the matter with him?"

"I was sayin' a while back," answered Lefty, "that he took and ate out of the hand of Silvertip. That's all that I was sayin'. He was right friendly with Silver."

"He was dead beat, and he couldn't help what he did," argued Chuck.

"He took and ate out of Silver's hand," said Lefty.

"What's the idea? Was that crook of a man-killer—was he any better than us?" demanded Chuck.

"I was just thinkin' about Parade eatin' out of his hand," said Lefty dreamily.

His friend glared at him.

The main thing is right here in this," said Chuck at last. "Can we get Parade in shape to run him in the big race?"

"At the rodeo?"

"Yeah, at the rodeo."

"I dunno," said Lefty. "He ain't hardly got ambition to eat his oats. How would he come to run in a race?"

"We could stick a shot of somethin' into him," suggested Chuck.

"Yeah, we could do that," said Lefty. "But he'd have Brandy to beat, and I guess there ain't any hoss beatin' Brandy. He's a thoroughbred."

"Nothin' that ever lived," said Chuck, "could beat Parade. Everybody knows that."

"Not on a fifty-mile run," answered Lefty. "Not out there in the desert. But he ain't made for a one- or two-mile sprint. There's too much of him to get goin'. Who's this old codger?"

"It's Charlie Moore, that's been takin' care of Brandy a long time. Hello, Charlie."

Charlie Moore came slowly up to them, smiling vaguely.

"Gents," he said, "I been fired by Mr. Richmond. Seems like him and Brandy don't need me no more. I was wonderin' could you use me to take care of Parade?"

"What should we need of a man to take care of that hoss? Ain't we got a pair of hands apiece and ten minutes a day to work on him?" demanded Chuck.

"All right," said Moore. His vague old eyes steadied on them for a moment. "I just sort of cottoned to him, was all. And ten minutes ain't hardly enough to polish the hoofs of a horse like Parade, was all I was thinkin'."

He turned and went slowly out the door.

"Maybe we missed somethin'," said Lefty. "Maybe *he* could wake up Parade better'n a shot of dope."

"You talk like a fool today," said Chuck. "Leave off your thinkin', and let's have another drink."

CHAPTER XVIII

THE OLD STALLION

In the evening of the day, as soon as the stream of visitors stopped flowing up onto the platform—at twenty-five cents a head—in order to see Parade and the old mare, the canvas screen that turned the corral into a showroom was taken down, so that the wind might freely blow across the pair of captives. And on this evening, Parade and Mischief stood head to shoulder, she facing away to the northwest, the direction of the Sierra Blanca,

97

and he looking in the opposite direction, into the pen where Brandy was kept. The sun was hardly down; it was still flinging up an abundance of fire that clung to the clouds in red and gold, and it would be long before the twilight ended. This is the time when cowpunchers lounge, between day and night, and forget the hard day, and try to make every moment an eternity before it is necessary to go to bed again—which means one step from breakfast and the saddle.

"I can see all the peaks of the Sierra Blanca," said the old mare.

"All of them?" asked Parade sadly.

"All white and blue against the red of the sky—it's as red as firelight shining on smoke."

"Can you see old Mount Blanco, itself?" asked Parade.

"I can see it clear to the shoulders," said Mischief, "and below that it turns blue and melts into the other mountains."

"If we had gone up there, into the ravines," said Parade, "then, perhaps, they never would have run us down."

"You can feed on regret like moldy hay," said Mischief, "but it will give you indigestion and pain, afterward."

"Perhaps it will," said Parade, "but what else is there to think of?"

"Think of the time to come," said the mare. "Prepare for the moment when you may be able to strike one blow for freedom. Be like a coiled snake. It's better to die trying to get back to the Sierra Blanca than it is to live a slave all the days of your life."

"That may be true," said Parade, "but even if we escaped, he would come again and walk us down."

"You said that and you meant it," said the mare, "but you saw him fall dead."

"Yes," said Parade.

"And there is no other man in the world who ever tried to do such a thing as he managed. Now that he is gone, there is no other."

"You want me to play the king again," said the stallion. "I know the ways of the business now. That's true. I've learned how to shoot the bar that holds a gate, even. I could open this big gate here, for that matter, except that besides the bar there's a padlock on the outside. And if I were free, I could gather the best horses from the

98

ranches, I could go and raid their corrals and their ranges, and run off with what I want. But there's no heart in me to do these things, mother. Man would come again. The Great Enemy would find me; I would fail; I would be hunted down."

"I can see the other mountains fading," said Mischief. There's only one mountain left for me to remember, and And that's the way with my memory of this life, Parade. I have thought you were a king, but I was always wrong. There's only one mountain left for me to remember, and that is your father. He was the king!"

"You said," answered Parade, "that Man simply walked down into the valley and led him away. At least, I fought harder than that!"

"It's not by reins and saddles and spurs and ropes that men control some of us," said the mare, "but Man puts his will on some of us, and then we can never escape. And your father was raised by a man he loved. He used to talk to me about the touch of his hand and the magic of the voice. I heard that voice calling out to your father, and he could not move. But if he had been raised wild and free, like you, Man never would have been able to break his heart as your heart has been broken!"

"Tell me more about the mountains," said Parade. "Can you see them now?"

"Only Mount Blanco, and the blue is growing up from the earth and covering it more and more; now to the shoulders, and the summit is all that remains, like a white cloud. Look for yourself."

"I'd rather hear about the mountains than see them," said Parade. "I look down at the ground all day long, because when I see the Sierra Blanca in the distance, I begin to think of the great days, and of the great runs, and I can taste the water of every water hole, and the grasses, and the tips of the shrubs on the foothills. But most of all, how we left Man struggling behind us, like little foolish pools of dust that the wind has raised and then run away from."

"You can think of those days," said the mare, "but still you haven't the heart——"

"You never passed two days staggering up the Salt Creek," said Parade. "If you had, you would have left your heart on the ground there. Hush! The old stallion in the next corral wants to talk to us."

"Let him talk to himself," said Mischief. "I'm tired of horses. I want to be alone. Ah, the day you were foaled, when I looked at you and saw you leading all the herds in the world, blackening the valleys, sweeping over mountains—but there is only one horse, after all, and he is dead —or so old that death is only a step from him."

She moved off to a far corner of the corral, and Parade went to the fence, and touched the nose of the old horse, half of whose head was reached through the bars.

After touching noses, they went through the rest of the formal greeting which two well-bred horses always exchange. That is to say, they withdrew half a pace from one another, tossed their heads high, stamped, and returned to look at one another with bright, half-mischievous eyes.

"I have watched you and heard your voices," said Brandy, "and there is something about your companion that reminds me of the one happy moment of my life, long, long ago. The one really happy moment, because it was the one free moment."

"Have you been free?" asked Parade.

"There was a time when I ran free," said Brandy. "That was longer ago than a colt like you could remember. But let me tell you, I have not always been like this, with staring hips and gaunt withers, and a scrawny neck, and sunken places over my eyes. Before Time had moth-eaten my coat, I shone almost as you do. Well, it's a foolish business to boast about the past!"

"It is," said Parade. "I have seen the time when a hundred horses followed me, and the men who hunted us might as well have hunted a flock of wild hawks in the sky. But those days are ended, and now I'm like you— a beaten drudge, a slave of man."

Suddenly Mischief came across the corral and stood at the side of Parade.

She said to Brandy: "There is something about you that reminds me of an old companion of mine. I wish that I could hear you neigh out with your full voice. I think it might have a meaning for me."

"There is nothing for me to neigh out loud about," said

Brandy. "Not unless I fall to thinking of the past, and that's a melancholy business."

"And what do you think of most in the past?" asked Mischief.

"One glorious time on which I don't dwell," said Brandy. "And for the rest—I'm a race horse, you see. And I think of races. I wonder if either of you ever faced the barrier?"

"I don't know what it is," said Mischief.

"A webbing," said the old stallion, "and the other horses stand beside you. The youngsters are on tiptoe. You can hear the crowd of people screaming higher and higher. The starters are trying to get the horses perfectly in line. The webbing flies up. There's one deep groan from all the people—and the race is on. And every start is another pull at the heart. It makes me young to think of it."

"You're old," said Mischief, "to still be racing. Do you win, these days?"

"Age doesn't matter so very much, up to ten or twelve," said Brandy. "That is, it doesn't if your blood lines are right. So I'm told, at least."

"For my part," said Mischief, "I always hold that one horse is as good as another!"

"I didn't mean to hurt your feelings," said Brandy, "in case you don't happen to be a thoroughbred."

"Thoroughbred, fiddlesticks!" said the mare. "I can tell you that I've been on deserts where a silly thoroughbred, with his paper skin and his soft ways of living, would wither up in a single day."

"I've no doubt you're right," said Brandy politely. "I didn't mean to claim any superiority. We were simply speaking of——"

"Thoroughbred, my foot!" snorted Mischief, interrupting. "For my part, I'm a democrat, and I don't care who knows it. I never believed in an aristocracy, and in a free country, there's no place for one. You're a thoroughbred, are you? Your long legs and your narrow chest, I suppose. I'd like to see those long legs climbing among some of the rocks that I've scampered through. Oh, it would do me a precious lot of good to see you trying to haul yourself over ice-coated rocks in the middle of winter, to get through a frozen pass—or else starve on the desert side!"

"Hush," said Parade. "You're insulting him."

"Thoroughbred, is he?" said Mischief furiously. "Well, I never laid eyes on a thoroughbred in my life, that I ever had any use for—barring one. And that one didn't look like this poor, skinny wreck."

"Go off and leave us alone," said Parade. "You've disgraced us both."

"I'm glad to leave you," said Mischief, "though what you can find to talk about to a conceited, overbearing, rude, intolerant boor of a worn out thoroughbred, I can't tell."

With that, she stalked across the corral, and Parade apologized at once.

"The fact of the matter is," said Parade, "that it's a tender subject with her. But I'll tell you that the only horse she ever respected was a thoroughbred, who was my father."

"Was he, indeed?" said Brandy. "What were *his* blood lines, then?"

"You must understand," said Parade, "that my mother was a simple soul, and at the time she met my father, I dare say that she didn't know a blood line from a forty-foot rope."

"I understand you perfectly. She simply didn't ask," said Brandy. "And what a pity that is, because all thoroughbreds are more or less related. If you could dig down into your past, you might be able to find that you and I are cousins. My father was Single Shot, and my mother was Mary Anne; no, you wouldn't be able to place her very well, but, of course, you've heard of Single Shot?"

"No," said Parade. "I'm sorry to say that I haven't. I've lived away from race tracks."

"And a lucky thing for you," said Brandy. "There's no good comes to a young horse from such a business. I want to talk to you about it, but here's my friend, Man. I must go talk to him."

The rather bowed form of Charlie Moore was approaching the corral, his gentle voice sending a greeting before him.

CHAPTER XIX

SILVERTIP'S RETURN

CHARLIE MOORE OPENED THE GATE AND ENTERED THE small corral. He began to walk up and down, his hand lying against the shoulder of the thoroughbred, as Brandy moved beside him, led only by the pressure of that hand.

The mare said quietly to Parade: "There you see it! There's the slave that loves his slavery! *You* may be like that, one day!" she predicted.

"Never," said Parade.

Another figure loomed through the twilight.

"Moore!" bawled the voice of Harry Richmond.

Poor Charlie Moore started, and hurried out of the corral. He stood shrinking before Richmond.

"I told you you was fired," exclaimed Richmond. "What do you mean comin' back here in the middle of the night? Whatcha tryin' to do?"

"I was sayin' 'good-by' to Brandy," answered Moore. "That was all. I was goin' to say 'good-by' for the last time. It's quite a spell that him and me has been together."

"I don't wantcha no more," declared Richmond. "Get out, and stay out."

"I was goin' to say," muttered Charlie Moore, "that if you didn't want to pay me no more, I'd be pretty glad to go on workin' here for nothin', and takin' care of Brandy."

Another figure could be seen by Parade, moving dimly in the background of the dull light. The new man lingered beside a ragged mesquite, his outline blurring with that of the bush. He was within easy earshot.

"Hold on," exclaimed Richmond. "You ain't that kind of a fool, are you? You wouldn't work for nothin', would you?"

"I'd work for nothin'," answered Charlie Moore. "There wouldn't be much meanin' for life, if I lost Brandy for good and all."

He held out his hand in an unconscious gesture through

103

the bars of the corral, and the stallion put his soft muzzle against it.

"You'd work for nothin', and what'd you live on?" asked Richmond curiously. "Because I wouldn't be feedin' you. You can count that I wouldn't be wastin' no money on an old scarecrow like you."

"I'd manage somehow," declared Charlie Moore. "I dunno just how, but I'd manage somehow. I don't need much to eat. I'm getting sort of dried up, and I don't need much I could live on stale bread—and Brandy!"

He laughed a little, as he said this. Richmond laughed, too. He said carelessly:

"Well, if you're that kind of a fool, you can stay on. I don't particularly hanker after feedin' and curryin' the hoss every day. And I guess Lake don't, either. You can spend as much time with Brandy as you want."

He turned and went off through the twilight, and his loud, snarling laughter came trailing back behind him.

The man who had paused by the mesquite bush came slowly up. He stood by the corral that held Parade and Mischief, and Parade suddenly lifted his head high in the air.

"What is it? What's the matter?" asked Mischief.

"Can the dead come to life, mother?" asked the stallion.

"What nonsense are you talking about?" asked Mischief.

"It's he—it's the Great Enemy—it's he!" snorted Parade.

And he stood alert, like a horse at the start of a race, frenzied with eagerness to be gone.

"How are things, Charlie?" asked the voice of the stranger.

Charlie Moore whirled about.

"Hi! Silver!" he breathed.

They shook hands.

"It's he!" groaned Parade to the mare. "I know his voice. I could tell about him in darkness!"

"What if it is?" answered Mischief. "Does that mean you have to tremble like a foolish colt when it first smells green grass in the spring of the year? What is any man to you?"

"His hands never touched you!" said Parade. "He never

drew you back out of death into life. You never drank from the same water with him when thirst was killing you. Listen to his voice speaking! Doesn't it call to you? Don't you feel a madness to come to the touch of his hand?"

"Bah!" snorted Mischief. "The touch of his hand? I have no madness to come to the touch of anything except the good open wilderness of the Sierra Blanca."

"I'll come to him!" neighed Parade. "I'll jump the bars or break them down and come to him!" And his whinny rang long and loud across the night air.

Charlie Moore was saying: "It got so's Harry Richmond, he couldn't afford to keep me on, so he turned me off. I don't get no regular pay, no more. But I'm managing to keep along. Where you been, Silver?"

"Out in the Sierra Blanca."

"Have some bad luck? I see you got a bandage around your head."

"I had some—bad luck," admitted Silvertip. "You can call it that. Bad luck!"

He laughed a little, softly, and the neighing of the stallion broke in wildly upon his words.

"What's the matter? What's wrong with Parade?" murmured Charlie Moore. "Look at him prancin' up and down. Like he'd want to smash through the corral fence. What's drove him crazy?"

The neigh of the stallion shrilled through the evening like the shriek of a bagpipe and the thunder of a great brazen horn. It shook one's soul to hear that battle cry.

Up and down past the bars rushed Parade, swinging rapidly back like a caged wolf, now rearing, now beating at the fence with powerful hoofs, until it seemed that the barrier would surely be beaten down.

Lefty came running, yelling as he approached.

"There comes Lefty," explained Charlie Moore. "He's one of the two that caught Parade."

"One of the two that caught him?" said Silvertip. "I'm glad to know that. The other one was Chuck, eh?"

"That's right. You know 'em?"

"I know 'em," said Silvertip. "I'm going on, Charlie. I'll see you again tomorrow. In the meantime, remember that you haven't laid eyes on me. There's something that I want to do. Understand?"

"I understand," agreed Charlie Moore.

"You're broke, I suppose," said Silvertip, drawing back farther from the corral as Lefty drew near to the frantic stallion inside it.

"I got a quarter," said Charlie Moore. "I ain't broke."

"Here's five dollars," said Silvertip.

"I ain't worked for it," answered Moore. "I can't take it."

"You take it, and maybe I'll be able to show you how to work for it later on," said Silvertip. "So long, Charlie!"

And so he was gone, stepping quickly away through the night.

Lefty, in the meantime, was striking at the fence of the corral with a stick, and shouting and cursing Parade, but he might as well have called to a storm wind. Parade, every moment, grew still more violent, still rearing, still beating at the fence with his forehoofs, and sending his ear-blasting neigh across the night.

Chuck came. Others gathered. Lantern light fell through the bars of the corral and through the rising mist of dust that kept boiling up from the ground, showed Parade flashing here and there.

"It was that fool of an old Charlie Moore!" yelled Lefty. "He was out here. He done something to Parade! I'm goin' to take it out of his hide!"

Chuck went to Charlie Moore and grabbed him by the shirt at the throat and flashed lantern light right into the blinking old blue eyes.

"I didn't touch Parade," said Charlie Moore. "I wouldn't do nothin' wrong to a hoss."

"Who was out here talkin' to you?" demanded Lefty.

"A gent that come to look at Parade—but it was too dark to see nothin', and he went off."

They could get nothing from Charlie Moore, but they cursed him from their hearts and fell back upon the task of taming the fury of Parade.

Suddenly, it left him as it had come, in a flash.

He stood at the corner of the corral, facing steadily toward the direction in which Silver had disappeared, and the men, climbing onto the fence, looked down on him like explorers upon new lands.

"Something has happened," said Lefty, at last. "Look at him quiverin'. Look at his eyes. Look at the way his tail is standin' up. Look at the bend in his neck. By thunderation, that's the hoss that drove gents mad—the look of him—when he was rangin' through the Sierra Blanca. His heart's come back to him!"

"His heart's come back to him," said Chuck. "I guess he'll be quiet now, for a while. Maybe he smelled somethin'."

They left the horses to darkness.

Still, in the black of the night, Parade remained standing as before, looking out at the southeastern stars.

"What is it now?" said Mischief, at his side.

"Nothing!" said Parade. "He's gone, and there's nothing left. But somehow I'll find a way to tear down this fence with my teeth and hoofs and get out and follow him till I find him."

"You act," said Mischief, "not like a horse at all, but like some starved beast of a meat eater. I've never seen a horse behave like this, Parade. Not even your father when he was first tasting freedom and ranging the Sierra Blanca like an eagle in the sky. Lie down, be quiet, and remember that tomorrow is another day."

CHAPTER XX

THE SHERIFF TALKS

THAT NEW DAY BROUGHT THE BEGINNING OF THE RODEO. Parmalee, already overcrowded, was now filled to overflowing, and all day long the air was trembling with the lowing of cattle and the neighing of horses, the clashing of horns and the beating of hoofs, until the very earth seemed to come to life. It was early in the morning when Lefty and Chuck brought saddle and bridle to the corral where their stallion was housed. They found Parade wandering restlessly up and down the fence, hunting ceaselessly, hopelessly, for a means of escape.

"It wasn't no shot of dope that was shoved into him," said Chuck. "It wouldn't 'a' lasted this long, Lefty. If this here hoss has come to life, we're goin' to have a chance of doin' somethin' with him in the rodeo race."

107

"Agin' Brandy there?" Lefty sneered.

"We could bet on him for second place," answered Chuck.

They entered the corral, unnoticed by the stallion. Lefty roped him; Chuck saddled and bridled him, and mounted.

He had barely settled into the saddle, he had barely gathered the reins, when the horse beneath him exploded with incalculable savagery. It seemed to Lefty that the air was filled with a dozen images of that horse and rider. Then Chuck was hurled from the saddle and sent crashing against the fence. His head struck a post; his loose body thumped against the ground.

Lefty dragged out the senseless Chuck beneath the lowest bar of the fence. He dared not enter while the maelstrom continued to rage. Mischief was backed into a far corner, pressing herself into as small a compass as possible, her legs bending under her with fear. Old Brandy had even retreated to the opposite side of his own corral. And still Parade fought, twisted, bucked, until the girths loosened and the saddle fell from him.

At the saddle he went with insane fury. With teeth and hoofs he battered it to a mere blur of what it had been. Then galloping with a ringing neigh around the corral, the loose ends of the reins caught over the top of a post, and the bridle was promptly ripped from the head of the big horse.

He was free, again, sweat-blackened and polished, flecked with froth here and there, magnificent beyond expression.

Lefty looked at that glory of horseflesh with a snarling lip, and then he glanced back at his companion.

The eyes of Chuck had just opened, and they were the glazed eyes of a very sick man.

"Shoot that killer," said Chuck. "He's smashed me up. I'm all broke inside. The life's runnin' out of me, Lefty!"

But the life did not leave the body of Chuck. They carried him—Lefty and two strangers who happened by—into the barn, and cared for him there. And when a doctor came, the man of medicine made a careful examination and reported that there was nothing to fear if Chuck were kept quietly in bed for a few weeks.

"He was almost smashed in twenty places," said the doctor, "but being tough stuff, he only bent instead of breaking."

Chuck was carried on a stretcher to the hotel, and put to bed. By the time he was installed in his room, Parmalee and all the crowds in it had heard the story of the return of the stallion to wildness.

A still more important thing happened to Lefty, as he left the hotel. For he saw a tall fellow walking down the street with a peculiar swing to the shoulders, and to Lefty it was as though he had seen a ghost moving in the open light of day. The figure turned a corner. Lefty saw the white streak of a bandage that passed across the forehead.

Lefty stood transfixed. He said aloud, finally: "If I'd only taken one more look—if I'd only listened to his heart —but I *seen* where that bullet busted right through his brains!"

He went into the bar-room and took three big whiskies in a row. By that time the fumes of them had reached his brain, and the crazy specter of fear was subdued a little. He could think for the first time.

A mere tap on the head with the butt of a rifle would have ended Silvertip, on that other day, when he lay prostrate, his arms flung wide, and his eyes slightly open, exactly like the eyes of the dead. But now he was up and alert.

It was only wonderful that he had not found Chuck and Lefty before this, and put bullets through them. Chuck would now escape—the lucky devil was confined to bed, and according to reputation, Silvertip was not the sort of a man to pick on a helpless enemy.

But he, Lefty, was not helpless! Not only was he up and about, but he carried with him his own reputation as a fighting man. Yet he knew the distance, the infinite gulf, that separated his talents from those of Silvertip.

When the whisky had brought some calm to his mind, Lefty went out to find the sheriff. It was walking in a new world, to go down that street hunting every doorway with his eyes, coming to every corner as though to the mouth of a cannon. But there was no sight of Silvertip, and so Lefty came at last to the office of the sheriff, a little one-room shack where that square-faced, savage man of the law lived by himself.

He was at his desk, laboriously writing a report. He looked at Lefty with bright, impatient eyes.

"I been and heard that your partner was laid out, Lefty," he said.

"That ain't why I'm here," said Lefty. His thin face grew thinner still, as it lengthened with gloom. "I'm here," he said, "because there's a gent on my trail that's goin' to get me before the day's out, I reckon. I mean Silvertip is back in Parmalee!"

"I know he is," said the sheriff. "I've heard that talked about, too. How come Silver and you to have bad blood between you?"

"It don't take no effort to make Silvertip start on a gent's trail," answered Lefty. "You know what he's done in the world. There's more'n twenty dead men scattered down his trail, and that's a fact. And them that they count are only the known ones. Maybe there's twice as many more that ain't accounted for."

The sheriff twisted his mouth to one side and grunted.

"When killin's get more'n five or six," he said, "I always start in and doubt 'em a good deal. You better do some doubtin', too!"

"It ain't the arithmetic that makes Silvertip dangerous, anyway," said Lefty. "All I know is that he's after my scalp and I ain't ready to lose my hair."

The sheriff began to rub his knuckles across his chin. "I gotta remark," he said, "that I been and talked to Silvertip some time ago and told him that I was watchin' him. I gotta remark, too, that for all I've ever heard of him, I've never heard of anybody sayin' that he went for his gun first."

Lefty sighed. He answered: "Look at here. Suppose that you was a bird. Suppose that you met a rattler. Suppose that you tried to get away, and the eye of that snake caught hold of you and held you tight. Why, you'd be swallered, the first thing you knew, and you wouldn't say it was a fair fight, no matter whether the snake made the first move or not."

"You mean he kind of hypnotizes gents?" the sheriff asked.

"Sure he does," said Lefty. "Not with his eyes, but with the rep that he's got. You take and look at him, and you can see the dead men in his face. If you look at his hands, you can see those hands wishin' the gun right out of the air. He can shoot quicker than a wasp can sting. And a man has no more chance agin' him than a spider has when a wasp up and sings in the air over it. The spider, he just lays down and gets ready to die. He's too scared to run. And that's the way with most of us when Silvertip is around. We know what he's done before; we know that he can do it ag'in."

"There's folks that have fought him," said the sheriff. "There's stories of plenty of folks that have stood up to him."

"Sure," said Lefty. "There was a good plenty of 'em in the early days before he got known. And even after that, there was gents that would get together, two or three of 'em at a time, and try their luck with him. There was the whole Harris family that jumped him up north in Montana. There was old man Harris and his five sons, and a coupla cousins throwed in. They cornered Silvertip in a box canyon, and he had to fight his way out. Well, old man Harris stayed behind in that canyon after Silver got out, and there's only four of the boys left, and most of 'em limp, or something. They used to raise a lot of trouble, the Harrises did, but now they're the quietest family in Montana."

The sheriff nodded. "I've heard tell of that fight," he said.

"What I want," said Lefty, "is to get Silvertip bound over to the peace, or somethin', while he's around this here town."

"There ain't anything to bind him over for," said the sheriff. "He ain't done nothin', and he ain't said nothin'. Not that nobody has heard. But I'll go and give him another talkin' to. What's this I hear about Parade goin' and wakin' up and turnin' wild ag'in?"

"I dunno how it is," said Lefty. "Queer things is in the air. I've *seen* what Parade's turned into, but I dunno how it come about. I'm goin' to get that Mexican, Jaurez, to ride Parade and gentle him before the race."

"Jaurez can ride anything that wears hair," said the sheriff. "He'll tame Parade, all right. But you ain't goin' to win much out of that race, Lefty—not if Parade was twice what he is. It's a shame to put him into a race like that. It ain't more'n a mile and a half, and he couldn't stretch himself out and get warmed up in that kind of a run. It needs one of these skinny, spindlin' thoroughbreds to sprint a race like that. Like Brandy is, maybe. And besides, there's a gent here that calls himself Steve Jones, and he's got a long, narrow, washed-out lookin' chestnut mare with him—and if he ain't a jockey, and if she ain't a ringer right fresh off the big tracks, I'm a sucker. You keep Parade right outta that race. If he had the lot of 'em out in the desert, he'd run their hearts out three times a day, but a race track is different."

He left the office at the side of Lefty.

"I'll find big Silvertip," he said, "and I guess he won't make no trouble while he's around here."

He found Silvertip, in fact, sitting in the long line of loafers whose chairs were on the veranda of the hotel, tipped back against the front wall. He beckoned the big fellow to him, and Silvertip came down into the street. He was making a cigarette and he offered the tobacco and wheat-straw papers to the sheriff.

The sheriff refused them with a gesture.

"You're here after Lefty," said the sheriff. "Is that right?"

Silvertip smiled.

"You're here after Lefty," said the sheriff. "It ain't me alone that knows it. Understand what I mean, Mr. Silver?"

Silvertip lighted his cigarette.

"Silence ain't goin' to do you no good," said the sheriff, raising his voice angrily. "I'm givin' you warnin' right now to get out of this here town. Move on, and leave Parmalee, and stay out of Parmalee. Hear me?"

Silvertip smiled again.

At this, the sheriff took half a step back. There were many eyes watching him, and he could understand that he was being quietly, silently tested in the minds of all those men who beheld him. Something was demanded of him, some sort of action.

But what could he do?

He could not, after all, pick up Silvertip on a charge of vagrancy. He had ordered the man to leave Parmalee, but since there was no charge against him, he could not force him to move on if Silvertip were minded to resist. He looked up at the white bandage around the brow of Silvertip. He looked beneath that bandage at the face which had been recently reworked in deeper lines, and with a finer, closer modeling. It was not the same man to whom the sheriff had talked not so many weeks before. It was a new soul, incased in flesh which had altered, also. The steel had been given a finer tempering; it possessed a sharper and more remorseless edge.

"I've told you," shouted the sheriff suddenly, "that this ain't the town for you. Get out!"

It was the crisis. The men along the veranda of the hotel leaned forward, or slanted to one side, and all narrowed their eyes to make sure that they observed every particle of this historical event.

They saw the right hand of Silvertip slowly convey the cigarette to his lips. They saw the end of the cigarette turn red with fire; they saw it lowered; they saw the lips of Silvertip part a little, and rippling tides of white smoke drawn inward, disappearing; and with the exhalation, they saw the cloud of smoke blown with careful aim straight into the face of the sheriff.

The sheriff did not move until every whit of that smoke had been blown in his face. Then the others could see that he was gray and drawn and looking weary, as if with a burden of new years laid on his shoulders.

At last he said: "All right, Silvertip. You've called my bluff. I ain't man enough to lick you. I swaller this insult, but the minute that you step a quarter of an inch across the line of the law, I'm goin' after you. Every man has gotta die once, and I reckon that my time is pretty close to up!"

CHAPTER XXI

JUAREZ, THE HORSE BREAKER

IN THIS SINGULAR SCENE, IT WAS FELT THAT BOTH MEN had come through the crisis with undiminished reputations. Silvertip, without lifting a hand or speaking a single word by way of threat, or doing anything that would have, in a court of law, more weight than a puff of smoke, had quietly defied the sheriff and all that the sheriff represented.

113

The sheriff, on the other hand, had endured the strain of a superior force without weakening, and a great deal of sympathy and respect were felt for him, accordingly.

After that meeting, half a dozen men went to the man of the law and quietly suggested that they would make themselves into a committee to look after Silvertip while he was in Parmalee. The sheriff promptly swore them in as deputies, and they went off to find their man.

They found him where the rest of Parmalee was to be found—out at the rodeo grounds where Parade was to be ridden this day by Jaurez. Everyone in town knew by this time that the stallion had suddenly gone wild again, and that the real Parade was now to be seen, as he had been when he reigned over the Sierra Blanca. And the six deputies, ranging quietly up beside big Silvertip, found him staring toward the shed out of which the stallion would be brought into the big inclosure. He was rapt. The coming of the deputies seemed to mean little or nothing to him.

And now all other matters were forgotten by every man and woman and child in that crowd, for out of the shed, and through the gate into the rodeo grounds that occupied all the ground inside the race track, burst Parade.

He came as if he wished to exemplify his name, rearing, plunging, swerving like a bright sword blade. Two cowpunchers with strong lariats and competent horses were controlling him, but he seemed to be dragging them along as though they were stuffed toys. He was a thunderbolt newly forged and polished, and every heart shuddered, and every heart leaped, at the thought of sitting on the back of that monster.

Lefty was one of the cowpunchers. He had Parade take the complete circuit of the field, inside of the big fences, and when he came opposite the benches which had been built under a shed and which were called the "grandstand," he made a little speech.

"This here hoss," said Lefty, "has pretty near killed my partner. When I seen him skyrocket, I figgered that there was hardly no other man that would be able to set him out. But Jaurez thinks he can do it. He's bet me a hundred dollars that he can; and I've bet him three hundred that he can't. Jaurez, if you're anywheres about, step out and show yourself, because Parade is plumb ready!"

It seemed as though Parade exactly understood that speech, or perhaps it was because he could see the far-off peaks of the Sierra Blanca shining like spear points against the sky. At any rate, his head went high, his tail swept out in a loftier arch, and his neigh sounded like a trumpet of challenge across the field.

There came to answer it a tall Mexican, who slithered through the bars of the fence, and went on, carrying a saddle and a bridle. His face would have been handsome, but smallpox had ruined it as life had ruined the soul of the man. Existence was to him a sneer. The years had battered him. He walked with a slight limp, but in his mouth and in his eyes he expressed his contempt for the world.

At this moment, he made a splendid picture for mind and eye, as moved out across the field toward the savage beauty of the golden stallion. For an instant, everyone forgot what was known about Jaurez the savage, and saw him only as Jaurez, the peerless horse breaker. Some men were accustomed to say that after Jaurez had broken a horse, not even a veterinary surgeon could put the poor beast together again. He was known to have ridden twenty famous outlaws until their hearts were gone, and though he had had his falls, as his limping proved, still in the end he was always the conqueror. But it was felt that now he was going to meet as fair a test as ever would be found.

It was the sort of a contest that the West has always loved—man against nature, with the dice loaded on nature's side, for when the Mexican had reached the side of the stallion, he looked a mere wisp, a mere stripling beside the glory of Parade.

Parade was blindfolded by Lefty; the saddle and bridle were slipped on, and in a moment Jaurez was smoothly up and in the saddle. Lefty, his hand on the blindfold, was seen to speak for an instant to the Mexican. No doubt he was rehearsing the terms of the agreement—that the attempt would be limited to three falls. If by that time the stallion had not been mastered, then Jaurez lost his bet.

Jaurez was seen to agree to those terms with a slight gesture. Lefty, leaning from his own saddle, jerked off the blindfold. Parade sprang like a released fountain into the air.

There was something more than the hands of Jaurez to control him, in the last emergency, for with a sixty-foot rawhide lariat, Lefty still had a hold on the horse. But now he kept that rope slack, and allowed Parade to fight as though for freedom.

And Parade went mad.

Have you seen a cat fly into a passion because it loses the mouse with which it has been playing? Have you seen it bound here and there, striking, and leap into the air, and hurl itself down, rolling over and over? So Parade turned his great body into the body of a cat, and seemed to grip the earth with claws.

And there was this blood-curdling factor of interest, that with every twist and turn and fall, he was continually striving to put teeth or hoofs on the Mexican. He wanted to get that burden off his back, and once off, he wanted to smash the life out of it.

The thing was appalling. The women began to look down at the ground. Children opened their eyes and their mouths. And even of the men who thronged the fences, there was hardly one who could find voice.

What gave point to the awfulness was that Jaurez himself seemed to be daunted for the first time in his reckless life. His whole face was as white as the ghastly silver pockmarks that were cut out of it. He kept on grinning, but there was no life in the smile; it was like the grimace of the punch-drunk boxer who still keeps stretching his mouth toward a smile of indifference, as the blows make the hair leap on his head, and cause his knees to sag.

Jaurez, plainly, was afraid. He was a dozen times out of the saddle and onto the ground as that huge wildcat flung itself down and turned and twisted. And always he was back into the saddle again at the critical instant as Parade lurched up to his feet.

Then came the end. Everybody could see that it was coming. Parade began to leap at the sky and come down on one stiffened foreleg. It was wonderful that even whalebone and sinew like his could withstand such frightful shocks. And every time, Jaurez was snapped like the lash of a whip. His chin came down on his chest, or his head banged over on his shoulder. His sombrero went off. His hair exploded upward with every shock.

And then the red flag of danger showed on his face, as he started bleeding from ear and nose and mouth.

He was done. Men began to hold their breath and stare as though they saw a man toppling on the brink of a cliff. Up in the grandstand a woman was screaming in a terrible voice, calling out to shoot the horse and save Jaurez.

That was what everyone felt. Once Jaurez struck the ground, Parade would finish him. Parade would turn him into red pulp in one second, unless Lefty with his rope and his cow horse could manage to hold the stallion.

Jaurez was holding by spurs and hands. He was "pulling leather" for all he was worth, but nobody blamed him for that. He was in the center of a tornado, and fighting for his life. The quirt which he had swung so gayly in the beginning now hung down, flopping like a dead snake from his wrist.

Then human nature could stand no more of that punishment.

He knew well enough what lay in store for him if he were flung to the ground, and he determined to shoot Parade dead beneath him. One wild yell burst from all throats together, like a shout from a chorus when a conductor strikes down his baton; for everyone saw the flash of the revolver as Jaurez drew it.

The stallion seemed to see it, also. Instead of leaping at the sky again, he dodged cat-like to the side, and Jaurez sailed out of the saddle, diving at the ground.

He put a bullet into the dust, and then his body struck on the same spot. It was something like throwing a stone into the water and then diving at it. People spoke about that, afterward.

And Parade?

As he whirled to dart back at the fallen man, Lefty did his part well and nobly. He threw his cow pony back on its haunches and jerked the lariat tight. The poundage of the stallion hit the end of that rope like a freight train going down a sharp grade. There was no more danger of that rawhide breaking than of a steel cable coming apart, but Lefty and his horse went over with a crash.

Lefty was flung far to the side, rolling; the horse rolled, too, and as the pommel of the saddle snapped, Parade came clear of the wreck with the length of the lariat streaming almost straight out from his neck.

That was the speed with which he was hurling himself forward, and he went straight at the fallen body of Jaurez.

No man would ever forget how Jaurez, stunned and broken as he was, turned like a worm that has been half crushed under foot. He still had his gun in his hand, and now he fired it twice, right at the charging stallion.

He missed. Almost of course he missed, for his hand must have been shaking and his eyes half blind. Then the Colt went wrong. The hammer dropped, and there was no explosion to answer its fall.

The stallion was almost on the fallen man by this time. Around the fence, perhaps a hundred men had drawn their guns, when a very odd thing happened. One voice broke out above the tumult in a great, wordless cry, and as Parade heard it, it seemed to strike him like a volley of lead.

He plunged suddenly to the side, veered off in a circle, and then started once more for his victim.

Poor Jaurez had turned again. He was trying to drag himself on his hands toward the fence and safety. The lower part of his body dragged like a limp sack behind him. He had his face turned over his shoulder, watching the rush of Parade, and he was screaming. Other voices were shrieking, too, and all the screams did not come from women, either.

Those poised revolvers along the fence were about to come into action with a roar that would have blown Parade into kingdom come, but the shooting was stopped by a stranger thing than any man ever had seen before. For a big fellow with a bandage about his head came running out straight toward Parade.

It was suicide, but it was such dramatic suicide that people forgot even about Jaurez and fastened their minds on this madman.

What they saw was Silvertip standing astride Jaurez, and Parade hurtling down on him. Silvertip put out a hand, and incredulous eyes saw that there was no gun in that hand. It was open. The palm was turned up. The fool seemed to be treating this equine tiger like a friend.

What actually happened was that Parade sheered off at the last instant. He turned around and around that motionless central group, where Jaurez now lay flat with his face in his hands, shutting out the sight of destruction, and where Silvertip kept moving just enough to face the wild horse.

Then Parade put on the brake by skidding all four hoofs through the dirt and coming to a halt in front of Silver.

The horse put up his head and sent his ringing neigh across the field and through the stunned brains of the spectators. They could see that the hand of Silvertip already was caressing the polished neck of Parade!

That was not all, but that was the picture which remained when everything else was finished.

There was the carrying of Jaurez off the field, and the long wait before the doctors announced that he would walk again—but never ride horses any more!

Then they had picked up Lefty like a limp sack, but all he needed was a dash of water in his face, and a slug of whisky down his throat. He came to, and could not understand, with his stunned mind, the strange story which men were trying to tell him.

These things had their interest, but what were they compared with the manner in which men saw Silvertip mount Parade and ride him with loose reins across the field, leaning forward in the saddle, keeping his hand on the neck of the great horse, while Parade turned his head a little, as he jogged softly on, and listened, and listened, and seemed to understand?

CHAPTER XXII

LEFTY'S PROPOSITION

WHAT BROUGHT BACK THE FULL USE OF HIS WITS TO Lefty was the information that Parade had been ridden away by Silvertip. He cried out in an agony that the horse was gone forever, and rushed out to pursue the trail.

Six good citizens of Parmalee went with him, and the sheriff was also in the group. They had changed some of their opinions about Silvertip since they saw the manner in which he had handled the horse, but if he had stolen

Parade—well, it might be a long trail, but they intended to undertake it.

What was their amazement when they traced Silvertip straight back to the corral where Parade always had been kept by Chuck and Lefty? And there stood Parade, now, with Silvertip beside him, rubbing the sweat out of his hide with twists of hay, and bringing up the true golden color.

They stood outside the fence, all of them, and stared. Then the sheriff went quietly away; his posse followed.

But before he left, the sheriff said to Lefty:

"You've been wrong about that hombre. There ain't any killing in his head, or he would 'a' left Parade to polish off Jaurez and bash in your own head. We're goin' to watch him, still—but I guess you're wrong!"

Lefty himself remained by the fence. He was trembling with excitment. He was terribly afraid, and yet he could not drag himself away from the spectacle of that horse which had changed so suddenly from tame to tiger, and back to tame again.

"Silvertip!" exclaimed Lefty.

"Well?" said Silver, without turning.

"It's this way," said Lefty. "Either you're goin' to go after my scalp, or you ain't!"

Silvertip said nothing. Lefty wiped the water from his forehead and flicked the drops from his fingers into the dust. They fell in thin, straight lines of darkness.

"Silver," said Lefty, "the fact is that that hoss waked up and got wild after seein' you. Ain't that the fact?"

Silvertip went on with the grooming of the stallion, silently.

"I'll tell you what," said Lefty, "after what I seen today, I ain't goin' to try, ever, to ride the devil. Nobody else will try, either. He wouldn't be no good to me except as a show hoss, nor to Chuck, neither. What I wanta do is to make a proposition to you. You ride that Parade in the rodeo race, tomorrow, and you'll sure win it. And if you ride, I'm goin' to bet my socks on him. And if you win, Silver—why, you take the hoss, and that's that! Is it a go? He wouldn't be any good to me, anyhow!"

Silvertip, at last, raised his big head slowly. Then he turned toward the fence. With his hand, he kept on automatically stroking the stallion's brightening side.

"Have you seen that mare, that ringer, that the tough

little mug called Jones has brought into town, Lefty?" he asked.

"Yeah. I've seen her. She looks like she could split the wind," agreed Lefty.

"And there's old Brandy right here beside us. He can still move," went on Silvertip.

"He can," said Lefty, "but there ain't nobody that seen Parade move today, that don't think that he can beat the world, if there's a man to ride him."

"There's two hundred pounds of me, Lefty," said Silvertip. "Mind you," he added in a different voice, "I'm going to have Parade one of these days. If I have to wipe out the murdering pair of you, I'll do it. Because I'm going to have Parade."

The calmness with which he spoke did not deceive Lefty, and the tremor of mortal fear went through him again. But he said, still sweating violently: "Look at it my way, Silver. You got an easy chance to get Parade, if you'll do what I say. There ain't no murder in it, if you'll do what I say, and we'll all have a chance to clean up. I'll clean up the coin, and you'll get Parade."

Silvertip looked aside at the horse, and the stallion turned his head and stared into the mysterious face of Man.

Silver sighed.

"It's no use, Lefty," he declared. "Suppose that I ride him? My weight would kill him. Besides, he's not meant for sprinting. I wouldn't shame him by letting him be beaten. If you want a match against Parade, take anything in the world out into the desert and then run 'em against Parade, and he'll laugh. But a race track sprint, that's a different matter. That chestnut mare—she can move. I know her lines, and they're meant for speed. Jones is a featherweight in the saddle on her. And Lake is not much more on Brandy. Parade would be giving them seventy pounds. He couldn't do it. No horse could do it."

Lefty looked from the man to the horse. It seemed to him, suddenly, dwarfed and deformed as his soul was, that he could see a similarity, a sort of kinship between the two; the same lordliness about their heads, the same calm fearlessness in their eyes, and something formidably big and wild about them both. Now that he saw the picture from this angle, it seemed to Lefty not strange that the

121

man should have won the horse, but that it would have been mysterious indeed if that kinship had not worked out.

"Silver," said Lefty, "I ask you this here—ain't it worth the try? Ain't it worth it? I'll make a few thousands if Parade wins, and you'll get Parade himself. Look at it that way, and figure it for yourself!"

"And what about Chuck?" asked Silvertip. "How does he come into the deal?"

The narrow face of Lefty sneered.

"Never mind Chuck," he said. "He got himself smashed up, and he ain't in the game, no more."

Silvertip looked the little man over carefully. Suddenly he nodded.

"I'll take the chance of shaming Parade for the chance of owning him," he said.

"Now you're talkin'!" cried Lefty. "I'm goin' to clean up on this. But listen to me, Silver—you gotta ride him till he's right in the palm of your hand. You better ride him today. Get him ready for tomorrow. It ain't long away —it ain't hardly long enough away for me to get my money down."

"I'll have him in the palm of my hand when the race comes around," said Silvertip. "Go off and lay your bets!"

He turned again to the grooming of Parade, which he continued till the big horse was dry.

He left, and again Parade began to move restlessly up and down behind the fence, whinnying, stamping at the ground, sometimes rearing and striking at the bars with his forehoofs.

The old mare, Mischief, came out of her corner of the corral, where she had been standing sullenly, and muttered at him:

"What's the matter, now, Parade? Why are you stamping and raging? He'll come back. You can depend on that. Men will keep on returning like winter. The great heavy brute! I'm thankful that I don't have to carry him on my back. Why are you hysterical?"

"You have never found a man," said Parade. "But *I* have found one. You've never had a hand on your shoulder that seemed to lie on your heart, also. And you've never had a touch on the reins that ran into your blood. You've never heard a voice that made you feel free, even under saddle and bridle. But *I* have heard that voice."

Mischief began to nibble at one of the posts, breaking off splinters of the wood, and pretending that she had not heard, but she knew that her son had been taken away from her at last. She could dream of the great wild freedom of the Sierra Blanca, but she would have to dream of it alone.

And she remembered how the man had come down into the valley and taken Brandy away, by the mere sound of his voice.

The old stallion spoke suddenly from the next corral: *"I have heard a voice, also. I have known a touch, too."*

"Bah!" said the mare. "A fool will still be a fool when he's old, and so are you. Who cares what you've heard and what you've felt? But my son has been king of the Sierra Blanca! Why do you compare yourself with him?"

"The Sierra Blanca? I know it very well," said Brandy, patient under this abuse. "I've been there!"

"You've been there under a saddle or a pack," said the mare. "Who cares where you've been? Who cares a whit? Not I!"

"I care," said Parade.

He went to the fence and pushed his head a little between the bars.

"I'd like to hear what you did in the Sierra Blanca," he declared. "I'd like to know what you've seen of it."

"I have talked enough," said Brandy stiffly. "There is an old proverb—when the mare is angry, never talk to the colt."

He turned away as he spoke, and now the pleasant, husky voice of old Charlie Moore came toward him, singing, and the old stallion ran to the gate of the corral.

"A disgusting—shameful—degrading sight!" said Mischief. "To stand and wait for a man, like a dog! And you, Parade, storming up and down again, whinnying, dancing like a little fool in its first May days! What shall I think of you but shame?"

CHAPTER XXIII

THE CROOKED THREE

THERE WERE ONLY THREE MEN IN THE BACK ROOM OF the saloon, and they looked as sordid as the atmosphere of the place. There had been a lamp on the table, but now it was moved to an adjoining one, because not one of the three wanted too much light to play over his features. The liquor in the whisky bottle was black, with one trembling highlight in it, blood-red, and in the glasses the drink appeared dull amber. They nursed these glasses with their hands, slowly turning them, drinking, not to one another but out of turn and out of order, their mouths twisting into sneers as the terrible bar whisky burned its way home.

Richmond was one of them, his swollen face creasing and dimpling as he spoke. The frog-faced half-breed, Lake, sat beside him, rarely talking. And opposite them was a lean little brown-faced man, that certain "Mr. Jones" who had brought to the rodeo the chestnut mare that looked fit to cut the wind like a knife.

Mr. Jones talked with a certain amount of dry humor, and frankness.

"You take birds like us, that've been barred off the tracks," said he, "and we can't pick and choose. We gotta enter our nags where we can, and pick up a livin', one way or another. That mare of mine has worn fifty different names in fifty different races. She's worn three or four different complexions, too. She's been a bleached bay, and she's been a red-brown. She's had all black stockin's, and she's had 'em all white. But no matter how she's dressed, she always runs like a lady."

Lake, at this, grinned down into his glass and suddenly sipped at the contents. Richmond lifted his big head and turned his fat face from side to side, making sure that there was no one near enough to overhear these confessions.

"It ain't any use to cry over spilt milk," said Richmond. "But I'll tell you something worth more than that old sayin'."

"Fire away," said Mr. Jones.

"It ain't any use *talkin'* about spilt milk, either!" added Richmond.

Jones put back his head and his leathery, thin face convulsed in silent laughter.

"You look scared enough for the prison shakes," he said. "Ever done time, Richmond?"

Richmond scowled at the words. "Whatcha mean by that? Time? Sure I never done time."

"You never done time?" said Jones, still laughing a little. "No, I guess you never have. Some gents are lucky, like that. Sometimes it's more than luck; sometimes it's just brains. Somebody else does the job for 'em—blows the safe—or rides the crooked race!"

He was still laughing, but the laughter was only a pretense. It was apparent that Jones was as ready for trouble as a bird is ready for a grain of wheat.

Richmond, therefore, made a broad, sweeping gesture.

"Lemme just tell you somethin'," said he.

"You been tellin' me plenty, right up to now," said Jones, dropping his head a little, and looking up from under the brows.

"Lemme just tell you this," said Richmond. "You and me, either we can do business together, or we can't. And bar-room arguments, they don't buy you anything, and they don't buy me nothin', either. What do you say?"

"I dunno," said the other. "I dunno what you got in your head, brother. I dunno what your style is, yet, or how you sell on the open market."

"I get a pretty good price, maybe," said Richmond. But that ain't the point. Do we do business, or do we just finish off this drink and bust?"

"Either way," said Jones. "I don't care. I put my cards on the table, and I don't care a whoop. You do what you please."

"All right," said Richmond, and he pushed back his chair.

Jones sneered down at his glass of whisky and made no move.

"Wait a minute, chief," said Lake.

He put his hand on the arm of Richmond, and the big

man readily slumped back into the chair from which he was rising.

"Whatcha want, Lake?" he demanded.

"I was just thinkin'," said Lake. "You two, you oughtn't to bust up like this here. There's money for you two to make."

"There's bullets for us to get in the neck, too," said Richmond, "if anybody happens to see us in here together, tonight. They'll know that we're saltin' the race away for tomorrow."

"Sure they'll know," said Jones. "And who cares? Who wants to make crooked money without havin' somethin' to flavor it? I wouldn't steal a dime, if there wasn't a chance for me to get caught."

"That's right, too," said Richmond, stirring in his chair.

"I'm not backin' up none," said Jones. "If you wanta do business, all right. If you don't all right. I'm not backin' up none, is all I say."

"He ain't backin' up none. That ain't what you want—for him to back up, chief," suggested Lake.

"Sure it ain't," said the rancher.

He looked suddenly into the keen, small eyes of Jones, and said: "We could do business together, you fool."

Jones merely grinned. "You sound more nacheral, now," he said.

"I been nacheral from the start," answered Richmond. "The point is, this whole town is nuts about the race tomorrow. It's crazy about the race, ain't it?"

"Crazy? Listen!" suggested Jones.

He lifted his hand.

It was well past the hour at which Parmalee was ordinarily asleep, but this was a night of nights, and a steady uproar rose from the place, higher than the flying dust. In the street there were two big parties of whisky-maddened cowpunchers who were sweeping back and forth down the long street, yelling, shooting off their guns, whooping. And when either of these groups came near, the thundering of hoofs and guns, the screeches of the riders, made talk impossible. Afterward the wave of tumult sudsided, but it was always present in the air.

Besides these climaxes, there was a steadier undertone of noise that moaned and laughed and roared its way out of Parmalee. There were two improvised dance halls, with two very improvised orchestras blaring out tunes well out of date, and from those halls came the laughter, the waves of sudden outbreaks of heavy voices of men, or single, piercing notes of women; and again the silence would be so profound that one could hear, even across the street, even behind flimsy walls, the whispering of the many feet upon the floor.

"Crazy? I'll tell you the town's crazy for tomorrow," said Mr. Jones.

"If they got an idea that anything crooked was pulled in that race, they'd take us out of the saddles and hang us up," said Richmond.

"They won't take *you* out of the saddle," said Jones, sneering. "You won't be ridin'." He looked at Lake, and sneered again, and nodded his evil head.

"That's all right," said Richmond hastily. "They'll know that I was behind the hoss and the arrangin'."

"Well," said Jones to Lake, "how good are you, kid?"

"I can put the mufflers on," said Lake, "and you wouldn't know a thing. Besides, I've rode Brandy every race he run. What I mean, though—he *can* run."

"So can the mare," said Jones. "And I can ease her down to a whisper, and make it look like she was just plain played out."

"The thing to do," said Richmond, "is to put our money on the mare. Put it up to her, to win, and a little to place, because the favorite is goin' to be Brandy. The boys around here know Brandy. They've seen him win a lot, and the odds are goin' to be favorin' him."

"Some are bettin' on Parade," put in Lake.

"Yeah? The fools!" commented Richmond.

"I seen the big guy out on Parade today," said Jones. "That nag can gallop."

"Silvertip is the only man in the world that can ride him, and Silver weighs two hundred pounds, and more," said Richmond.

"Yeah," said Jones, "but that nag can gallop."

"The race is a mile and a half. No horse can carry two hundred pounds a mile and a half and beat Brandy," said Lake.

"No?" persisted Jones. "I'll tell you somethin' else. Silvertip is full of brains, and brains take off weight. Brains don't weigh nothin' in a race."

"Silvertip can go hang," said Lake savagely.

Mr. Jones licked his lips, and laughed. He filled his glass, sloshing off the whisky out of the bottle, and tossed off another drink. Then he laughed again loudly.

"You two birds are scared of Silver, ain't you?" And still he laughed.

Lake said, with slow emphasis: "Yeah, we're scared. Everybody's scared of him."

"Listen to me," said Jones. He lifted a crooked brown forefinger. *"I* ain't scared of Silvertip."

"Then you're just a plain fool," said Lake.

Richmond jerked his glance suddenly toward Lake and then back toward Jones. It looked as though Mr. Jones were about to draw a gun. He had half risen from his chair, and his eyes burned. But presently he settled back again.

"Maybe you're right," said Jones. "Maybe I ought to be scared of him."

"Sure you had oughta be," persisted Lake.

"Let it go!" commanded Richmond. "The thing to do is you and me declare the mare to win."

"She'd beat Brandy, anyway," said Jones. "She's younger, and she can go like the wind."

"She couldn't beat Brandy," said Lake calmly.

"Shut up!" ordered Richmond. He added: "The mare wins, and we split everything two ways."

"And me?" said Lake.

"I'll take care of you," growled Harry Richmond.

Lake turned on his employer a yellow, sour grin. "Yeah, you'll take care of me," he muttered.

"That's fixed," said Jones. "You can't bet agin' yourselves, so you hand me the money, and I bet for you."

"I have to hand you the cash," agreed Richmond slowly, and he drew out his wallet.

Then his hand paused. His face turned bright with perspiration.

"I give you the cash——" he muttered.

"When I play a game with a gent, I play the game," said Jones. "But I don't care. You can all go hang, for all of me!"

Richmond opened the wallet, took out three small bills, and pushed the rest of the money across the table.

"Listen," said Richmond. "It's everything I've got. I

128

used to have a ranch. All I got now is a mortgage—since I followed the racing business. This is the last that I could get together. Listen—put some down on the mare to place. We gotta make sure."

"I'll do that," said Jones. "I'll write down the bets and the odds. I'll show you the list, afterward, and we'll split everything two ways. You trust me?"

Richmond sighed. "Yeah, I trust you," he answered.

"Then there's Parade," said Jones. "We gotta fix Parade."

"Why, you couldn't buy Silvertip. You dunno what you're talkin' about," retorted Richmond. "You couldn't buy him. He's one of those honest fools. He'd kill himself sooner than turn a corner short. Besides, you don't have to think about him, unless that crazy stallion of Lefty's runs amuck and kicks the daylights out of the mare at the post. And that ain't likely."

"Parade can gallop," said Jones scowling. "I watched him, and I seen him gallop."

"He's got two hundred pounds up," argued Richmond patiently.

"Take off fifty pounds of that for brains," said Jones. "Silvertip ain't anybody's fool."

"Well—just in case," remarked Lake, "we could box him."

"That's what I mean," said Jones. "No matter what Silvertip may do at the finish, the mare and Brandy have got the early foot. The last half mile—suppose that the stallion comes along pretty fast—you and me, we box him. I guess I'll be on the rail, and we'll box him! Understand?"

Lake chuckled at that. "Whatcha think?" he demanded. "Understand? Sure I understand. I'll nail a lid right down over Parade; if he tries to sneak up between us. I'll ride wide of the mare, and get ready to box off, if he tries to slip through."

CHAPTER XXIV

OUT OF THE PAST

THE NIGHT WAS WARM AND PERFECTLY STILL, AND THE stars kept burning down closer and closer to the earth, until no man could keep them out of his eyes, and heads were sure to be lifted toward the zenith and the Milky Way.

Inside, not outside, the corral fence, Silvertip was putting down his tarpaulin, and then unrolling his blankets; Parade, near at hand, kept sniffing at everything. When the bed was made, he caught the edge of it with his teeth and tossed everything into confusion. Silver shouted at him. He fled across the corral and came romping back. His great eyes glowed bright through the starlight.

"Yeah, he knows you, all right," said Charlie Moore. "How come?"

"How does it come that Brandy knows you, Charlie?" asked Silvertip.

"There was a question of him livin' or dyin', a long time back," said Moore, "and a hoss ain't like a man. A hoss never forgets."

"Well," said Silver, "it was a question once of both of us going over the edge of a cliff—or both being saved. He was sliding, and I wouldn't let go my hold on him. I couldn't let go. Something inside of me kept saying that it was better to go together, or live together. I couldn't let go—and we had the luck, together."

"I know," said Charlie Moore. "You goin' to sleep out here all night?"

"I am. It'll keep Parade quiet. He raises the devil if I'm not around, and he needs to be himself tomorrow."

"Silvertip," said Charlie Moore, "I want to wish you luck. I'd sure like to see you win and get that hoss. But you know how it is—you know how Brandy can run, and you know what you weigh."

"I'm not thinking," said Silvertip. "I'm only praying,

130

Charlie. Let's not talk about it. It means too much to me. What are you going to do, old timer, after this race—if Richmond moves out of this neck of the woods? They say that he's broke, and that he may have to move. About all that's left to him is Brandy, and I don't suppose that he'll take you along with the horse."

"He wouldn't take me along," agreed Charlie Moore, "and what I'd do without Brandy, I dunno. You take a life like my life, there's been only one thing in it."

"Come along, Charlie," agreed Silvertip. "Back yonder, in the old days—there was a girl or two, eh?"

"Never no women," said Charlie Moore. "You see how it is? I didn't have no tongue to talk to 'em. You gotta have a tongue, to talk to a girl. She can't see you by what you do, same as a man can. She's gotta have talk. No, there never was no woman. There never was nothin' else, except days of work, and pay at the end of the month, and that sort of a thing."

"That's hard," agreed Silvertip. "But you've had your friends, Charlie."

"I've had you, Silver," said Charlie Moore. "I guess you smile at me, a good deal, but to be smiled at is a lot better than to be laughed at. You're the closest friend that I've ever had."

Silvertip could not answer. He wanted to say something pleasant, but pity choked him.

Charlie Moore went on: "There's only been Brandy. It seems like the time before I had Brandy, I didn't have nothin'. Come here, Brandy, and talk to me."

Brandy came rapidly across the corral and pushed his head out between the rails. The hand of Moore began to wander over the fine, bony head.

"And when Brandy steps out," said Charlie Moore, without bitterness, with a sort of calmness of acceptance, "I've been havin' a feelin' that I'd step out, too. Just a sort of a feelin', if you know what I mean, but I guess I won't. The days'll go on, one after another, like walkin' down a long road, with no home at the end of it. You know how it is, Silver."

"Aye," said Silver. "I know something about that."

"So long," said Charlie Moore. "Good night, Brandy. Run like a three-year-old tomorrow, you old tramp!"

He turned and disappeared into the darkness. Behind

him, Silvertip set for a time on his blankets, hugging his knees. Then he turned in.

He looked at the frosty brightness of the stars for a moment. He thought of the test which was coming on the morrow. He thought of Parade as his own horse, bearing him through a greater, a freer, a nobler life. His heart leaped, and yet a moment later he was soundly asleep.

A little after that, Brandy lay down, with a groan.

"So, so!" exclaimed Mischief. "That's the way with old horses. They can't keep their feelings to themselves. They have to grunt and groan and maunder, and make themselves disgusting and life ridiculous for everyone else!"

Brandy had endured much. Now he started lightly to his feet.

"I'm only about nine years old," said he, "and I can run within a step as fast as I ever ran in all my days, just now. Don't talk to me all the time about old horses. There have been horses three times my age, for that matter, before they died."

"Nine years of slavery!" exclaimed Mischief. "Nine long years of slavery!"

"I was once as free as any of you," said Brandy. "You can talk down to me, if you please, but I was once as free as any horse in the world."

"Were you?" The bitter mare sneered. "Free in a pasture—free in a corral—free in a stall—that's the only freedom you've ever known."

"You were speaking a time ago," said Brandy, "about the Sierra Blanca. Well, I ranged through that, one time."

"A very short time," said the mare.

"I wish it had been longer—except for the hand and the voice of the man I love."

"It sickens me to hear that sort of talk," said Mischief. "A precious lot Man ever did for me, except to feed a spur into my side and a Spanish bit into my mouth! You talk of love and Man? I can love my foal, and my free country, and that's the end—except for such a horse as the king of them all was!"

"And who was the king of them all?" asked Brandy calmly, because his disposition was able to endure worse spite than that of Mischief, even.

"The king of them all," said Mischief, "was such a horse as was only once in the world. How am I going to tell you about him? Imagine yourself! You're a good horse. You have lines, and bone, and you can gallop. Imagine yourself sleeked over, beautiful, and fast as the wind. Imagine yourself just escaping from captivity and running out into the desert for the first time. Imagine yourself on the sides of it. That's the sort of a horse I mean, and he was the king of the world, and he was the father of my colt here!"

"Well," said Brandy, "I can't imagine all of the things that you say, but I can imagine the time, well enough, when I got away from captivity, and ran out with a fine mare, a fine, wise, tough-minded, clever mare, right into the Sierra Blanca."

"You ran—with a mare—into the Sierra Blanca?" said Mischief.

"Yes."

She came slowly up to the bars, and sniffed at the head of Brandy. Then she asked:

"You went into the Sierra Blanca with a mare? What sort of a mare?"

"Oh," said Brandy, "she had run wild there. She had been wild-caught and she was still wild, on the inside."

"Come closer to me, Parade," said Mischief. "Come closer, and listen. Something is being told to us now. He escaped into the Sierra Blanca, and there was with him a mare that had been wild-caught off the desert—years before."

"Years before," said Brandy.

"Then tell me what happened after that!" Mischief demanded of Brandy.

"We came to a herd of wild horses, and there was a leader with them of course—a stallion."

"What color?" snapped Mischief.

"Cream-colored," said Brandy. "And I'll never forget how his tail flashed like metal, when he came sweeping around from the rear of the herd. And then——"

"Neither shall I forget!" exclaimed Mischief.

"You?" snorted Brandy.

"And how you fought, and how he caught you by the throat—and how you beat him to the ground, and then let him go! Parade, come closer to me! It is the king—it is your father! Time has marred him, but it is he. I should

133

have known him by his gentleness and his forbearance. It is the king!"

"What do you say to me?" asked Brandy.

He touched noses with her; he touched noses with Parade. Out of the past the wild days came over him, the wild and happy days when he had been a king indeed.

"And then a man came," said Mischief, "and called to you. When I was calling to you, too. I would have taught you how to run free, always! Why did you stand and wait for him to come?"

"You never will know," said Brandy. "But *he* understands!"

"Steady, boy!" called the voice of Silvertip suddenly, and Parade turned and went rapidly toward the blankets of the speaker.

"It is true," said Mischief. "But we have this moment. Here are the three of us. Now let tomorrow bring whatever it will!"

CHAPTER XXV

THE GREAT RACE

MEN BET THEIR PAST WAGES, AND THEIR FUTURE. MEN bet their spurs and saddles, and a saddle is the last thing that a cowpuncher places in jeopardy. Men bet with borrowed money, and with stolen money, too, for when a Westerner makes up his mind about the winner of a race, he makes it up with a violence, and with a perfectly firm conviction. They would have bet the skins off their bodies, if there had been money value attached.

And nearly half of those bets went down on Parade.

Common sense might say that the slenderer lines of the mare of Mr. Jones, and Brandy, meant greater speed over a distance as short as a mile and a half. But common sense is not the virtue of the great West. And when those cowpunchers looked upon Parade, his beauty and his fame joined in their souls and stirred their hands toward their pocketbooks to place their wagers.

There were plenty of others, calm and crafty-minded

people, who laid their money with what seemed greater discretion, and these bet on the "dark horse" of Mr. Jones, or on the celebrated speed of Brandy.

There were other entries, but they hardly counted. Eight horses danced and pranced at the post, with Silvertip towering head and shoulders above the rest, both on account of his own stature and the almost seventeen hands of Parade. Next to him was Brandy. And this strange thing was noticed even by the excited, abstracted eyes of the bystanders—that the two stallions actually touched noses more than once, in the intervals of fiddling for the start. But presently they were as wild as the rest of the horses. Only the long, rangy mare of Mr. Jones remained alert, but without wasting an effort, at her end of the line, and she was the farthest from the inside position.

As for Brandy, he was exclaiming: "We're going to run! We're going to race! Parade, try hard to keep close to me. I can feel the wind in my heels. I'm going to run faster than a storm. Stay as close to me as you can and try to be second. Watch the mare. She has the lines of speed, too. Watch the mare, and follow me, and you won't be disgraced!"

Then a gun boomed, and as the others lurched away from the start, Parade was left half-turned, standing flat-footed.

He got away like a wildcat, with the wailing cry of despair from his supporters ringing through the air.

He saw the mare sweep with wonderful speed right across the face of the field, and then settle down to the best position, on the rail, where she ran easily, with no effort, and kept the rest at bay. Brandy came up to her and looked her in the eye, and would have gone ahead, but the firm hand of Lake held him back.

"Make a race of it! Let her go!" called Lake.

There was nothing around them. The best of the range-bred horses were already laboring well to the rear, only able to fight it out for third-place money, and Parade was among them.

"There's plenty of time!" called back Jones. "Bear out a little, and watch Parade!"

"Parade's sunk already!" called Lake.

That was how they swept around the course for the first round. It was a three-quarter-mile track, and they would travel about it twice. And going by the little grandstand, where most of the people were thronged on the outside of the inside of the track, the voices rose up in waves, and smote the horses and riders in the face. There was the high, joyous staccato of the supporters of the mare and Brandy. There was the groaning despair of those who had bet on Parade.

He was out and away from the other range horses now, but a great distance from the leaders. And yet Silvertip was making no effort to urge him. He swung his body low along the neck of the stallion, like a jockey, and he had a high, strong grip with his knees, to keep his weight off the running muscles that come up under the saddle; but outside of position, and a firm but light grip on the reins, he was making no effort.

That was why they yelled at him. That was why some excited men called him a fool and a crook, and threatened to have it out with him after the race.

But he knew that whatever was in the body and the brain and the soul of Parade was his, and in his hand, ready to be poured out when he pleased. He told it by that electric current which quivered up and down the reins. He told it by the slight turn of the head of the horse, that showed Parade was studying his rider, waiting for him, ready for the supreme effort. And so Silvertip waited still. He was not exactly tense. It was something beyond tenseness, this pull on the strings of the heart, and this knowledge that he was riding for possession of the horse.

He remembered Lefty, pale-faced, keen, saying: "I've bet everything on Parade. Maybe I'm a fool, but I've bet more on you than on the nag. I don't have to tell you to do your best. You get Parade if you win!"

"And Chuck?" Silvertip had said.

"If Chuck opens his mug, I'll tell the true story—how Chuck put a bullet into you after you had Parade in your hand!"

That was how it would go—if he could win!

And little by little, as he hung quietly, in perfect balance, over the running machine beneath him, he saw that they were creeping up on the leaders—not rapidly, but little by little.

He knew it was unfair, this test. He knew that Parade

could maintain this speed for an indefinite time, and run the others into the ground if there were ten miles to cover. But what would happen when he asked for everything that Parade could give, and entered the stretch with the leaders—those narrower, clipper-built sprinters?

That would have to be seen.

They rounded into the back stretch, and Parade was coming closer up. Silvertip saw Lake turn his head—a single flash of that ape-like countenance, and then Brandy moved faster, and the mare moved faster beside him. Like a team, the mare and Richmond's stallion were keeping together, while the crowds went mad with excitement.

Not only the voices of their supporters, but now the majority of the men, who had bet on Parade, were beginning to yell also. For they saw the favorite creeping up with every stride.

The horses rounded the turn toward the head of the stretch, and then Silvertip set his teeth, and made his call.

The answer took his breath away. It was like leaping from a height. It was like being caught by the race of a river that is all white water. It was like being hurled from the hand.

The lurch of increased speed threw Silver back a little in the saddle. He had to struggle forward into the better position. And with that first rush, as they rounded the turn into the stretch, he came straight up on Brandy and the mare.

The two stallions jarred together. Brandy lagged; Parade, thrown completely out of stride, fell well to the rear, and the mare went winging on alone.

A screech of rage and disappointment went up from those at hand, along the fence, and murder flashed from the heart of Silvertip into his brain. They would die for this—Lake and Jones! He saw the plot as clearly as though he had sat at the table where it had been hatched.

And Parade? Could he come again, with that crushing burden on his back? Could he loose again that long-bounding stride, that seemed to be buoyed up by the beat of invisible wings?

He called, with his heart in his voice, and Parade answered. He swayed a little, but found himself, and shot ahead.

Brandy, running with wonderful strength, was beside

the mare again, but bearing well out toward the middle of the track, and the gap was plain and free before Silvertip. That was why he tried to put Parade through it, instead of passing around to the outside. It seemed impossible that Lake would attempt to foul him twice.

The finish was not far way. The two white-washed posts gleamed nearer and nearer. The frenzy of uproar did not come, it seemed, from human voices, but from wild beasts, and from blaring brazen trumpets.

Men were standing up on the rails, and pulling their favorites ahead with foolish gestures; and here and there someone with a weaker heart looked down at the ground, white-faced and overcome.

But the same rush of speed came pouring out of Parade, the same dazzling outburst as before. It would not endure long, this time. By a certain tenseness and brittleness in the body that labored beneath him, Silvertip recognized that fact.

Then he saw an odd thing, for as the ultimate strain was placed on both Parade and Brandy, as they stretched their heads out, they twisted them a little to the right, and bored into the wind of their own gallop, as though they were about to turn a corner. They were identical in style —and chance could not make this! There was only one great difference, and that lay in the greater sweep of the stride of Parade. It bore him rapidly up. The head of the stallion was on the hip of the mare, when suddenly Brandy was swiftly swung in again to close the gap.

It was too patent. Everyone in the stands, everyone in eyeshot along the fences could see the dirty device, and a howl of rage went upward.

But that was not what stopped Lake.

He would risk the rage of the crowd, knowing that every penny of money that Richmond possessed had been bet on the mare. He would risk everything, hoping to get his percentage, if only he could shut off Parade.

But now, as Parade came up, something happened in Brandy. The head which usually gave so easily to the slightest pull of the reins, now stiffened. The mouth became iron. There was a sudden outthrust of the neck of the stallion that tore the reins through the strong hands of the jockey, and Brandy was running straight and true toward the finish line, leaving plenty of space between him and the mare.

It was like the opening of a gate of hope, to Silvertip. The rage vanished from his heart.

He shouted again to the stallion. He saw the ears of Parade shudder as the horse heard the voice. He felt the final, desperate effort come out of the quivering body. That stride could not be made more rapid, and yet it beat more rapidly. That stride could not be lengthened, and yet actually it was extended!

The long, lean mare drew back in jerks. Those jerks represented the strides of Parade, one by one.

Then the sardonic face of Mr. Jones turned. He seemed not in the least degree excited. His whip worked rhythmically. Still something like a smile was on his face as he fell behind.

But the head of Parade was not in the lead. It was Brandy, running like a nimble-footed three-year-old, running as he never had run before, perhaps. Still his head was in front, while Lake, his frog face contorted, screamed out curses and plied the whip.

And then two great pulses, and Parade was ahead. The white posts flashed past. Had he gained that vital ground in time?

Silvertip did not know. It might still be Lefty's horse that he bestrode, he thought, as he turned back toward the grandstand. But then all doubt left him as men leaped over the fence or crawled through it, and came pouring toward him, and as they ran, they kept screeching out one name:

"Parade! Parade!"

There is only one sort of madness that pitches the voices of men as high as that, and that is the madness of victory.

Movement became almost impossible. The throng pressed closer and closer. In vain, Silver shouted to beware of the teeth and the heels of the stallion. The winners did not care. They wanted to touch that gleaming piece of victorious horseflesh if they had to die for it the next moment.

In a vast huddle, growing every moment, they attended Parade down the track.

Only one thing could part them, and that was a small man with a thin face and blazing eyes.

"It's Lefty—it's the owner!" men called, and gave place, meagerly, to Lefty.

He came up and gripped the right hand of Silvertip with both of his, and put his foot on Silver's, and so hoisted himself until he could speak in Silver's ear.

"I've made a fortune!" he shouted, "and you're goin' to have a share in it. You're goin' to have Parade, too. And welcome, too, because there ain't another man in the world worthy of settin' on his back. And it was the greatest race ever rode!"

CHAPTER XXVI

SETTLEMENT

ALL THAT LAKE COULD THINK OF, AFTER THE DEFEAT, was whisky. He went back to the same obscure little saloon which he favored, and took what comfort he could, until his eyes blurred, and his senses were dulled.

Afterward, Richmond would come—Richmond ruined, Richmond in a frantic rage. That would be that. Lake hardly cared. A savagery was in him. He had spent these years with Richmond, always waiting for the big clean-up and the time had never come. Now there would be some sort of a settlement.

The door opened from the rear, and Jones came in. He leaned over the chair of Lake to say briefly:

"Better get out of here. Richmond is clean nutty. He can't take it, the dirty welsher. You get out of Parmalee and stay out, or there'll be trouble. He thinks you double-crossed him. He can't see that Brandy took that race in hand at the finish. And what did I tell you? That Parade could gallop—and well he did!"

He laughed, his sneering, mirthless laughter, and went on into the front of the saloon.

He had hardly closed the door behind him when Harry Richmond came in from the rear entrance. Lake looked up askance, and saw the drawn gun in his hand, the big pulpy face thrust forward, the working of the mouth.

It was twilight. The fields and sky were blue outside the open doorway.

And this was to be the end. Lake knew it. He knew it by the fact that the light did not tremble on the gun of Richmond. The hand of the man was steady, and the murder would be done.

They said nothing. Richmond kept inching forward, his gun leveled. Lake got up from the table. He knew that the instant he tried to pull a weapon, he would be shot down. His own hand would give the signal for his death. But while he hesitated, Richmond was edging nearer, making sure of his aim, getting to a range at which he could not miss.

Suddenly the hand of Lake flashed across his coat and up under the flap of it. The Colt boomed in the hand of Richmond. A forefinger of fire stabbed through the murky air at Lake.

The shock of the bullet knocked him backward. He struck a chair. It went over with him. He turned a somersault and landed on his face with hands still clutching the gun he had drawn.

Richmond was still firing, and life was running out of the body of Lake with every throb of his heart. But he lay there stretched on the floor, making a rest of one hand to support the long barrel of the revolver. And from that rest he fired. After Richmond fell, he was not contented.

He wanted to get up and stand over the man and blow his face off. He wanted to crawl to him, and put in a final shot. But he knew that even the effort of getting to hands and knees would make the last of life burst out of him.

Even now, a dimness was being drawn across his face. The agony was entering his throat, closing off his breath. And still he fired.

Richmond began to shriek. He got to his hands and knees, screeching for help. Another bullet knocked him flat on his face.

There was no more firing, as the men broke in from the front of the saloon. Lake lay on his face, dead, smiling; and Richmond was two gasps from death, also.

It was only marvelous that he could exist long enough

to speak words, and Jones and the barkeeper leaned over him.

There was an expression of stunned surprise on the face of Richmond. His lower jaw had dropped to his chest.

He kept saying, thickly: "Tha's a'right. Tha's a'right," and a drool of blood spilled over his lip and kept sliding down on his coat.

Jones said, calmly, almost with enjoyment in his voice: "You're a dirty dog. You're dying like a dirty dog. But if you've got anything to put right, tell me, brother, and I'll do it for you!"

Harry Richmond looked up at him with vague eyes.

"Old Charlie Moore," he said.

Bubbles of blood formed and burst on his lips, snapping rapidly.

"Moore—he gets Brandy. I got Brandy away from him —and I got nothing but trouble. Give Brandy back to Charlie—and tell him——"

He put his head on his shoulder as though he wanted to wipe his bloody lips on his coat, but the head kept on sagging down, for Harry Richmond was dead.

When justice is done, sometimes it is not done with a feeble hand, but with a certain flourish. That was the case with Charlie Moore. The whole story came out. It had been known before, but dimly. Now the long story of injustices stood up darkly against the bright light of the race and the tragedy that had followed it. And Charlie Moore got Brandy.

He got another horse, too, because when Brandy was led out of the corral, Mischief tried to climb the fence and follow him. Big Silvertip bought Mischief on the spot and presented her to Charlie Moore.

Charlie was leaving Parmalee. He was going into the Northwest, where a comfortable job had been offered him as timekeeper in a big mine.

"Because," the mine owner had said, "the world's given the simple old fellow a bad break. Now he can have his horse, and peace, to the end of his life."

That mine lay on the edge of the Sierra Blanca, among the foothills, and Silvertip rode all the way with Charlie Moore to his new job.

What they said to one another made very little difference, but from horse to horse there was much talk. It was somewhat annoying to the riders because, while Mischief ranged here and there, without so much as a bridle on her head—it would be a simple thing to run her down, if she tried to bolt—the two horses insisted on walking shoulder to shoulder.

"You see," said Brandy, "that we return to the old places."

"We return," said Parade.

He lifted his head, and looked at the white spearlike tips of the Sierra Blanca range.

"Some day," he said, "perhaps we'll run together through the valley again, and gather a herd behind us."

"Never!" said Brandy. "To be free is a great thing; to be loved is a greater thing still. If there had been no whip on me, the other day, perhaps I would have beaten you, Parade, if I had loved my rider as you loved yours. Did he touch you with a whip, from the start to the finish?"

"A whip?" said Parade. "Why should he do that? A whip stroke only makes you twist to the side to escape from the pain. He never has touched me with more than the flat of his hand."

"And that," said Brandy, "I understand. But your mother never will. Where are you traveling now?"

"A great ways off," said Parade. "All I know is that with my master in the saddle, I keep looking at the horizon, because I know that he always wants to be somewhere beyond it. Look at him, father. He is the Great Enemy turned into a friend."

"Therefore," said Brandy, "you will be of one blood and one bone with him, all your life. See the man who rides me. He keeps a loose rein. His eye wanders. He trusts me, my son. And the greatest joy in this life is to trust and to be trusted."

And old Charlie Moore was saying to his companion: "Look at 'em rubbin' shoulders as they walk, rubbin' our knees together, too, the old fools. Now, I'll tell you somethin', Silver."

"Fire away," said Silvertip.

"You seen them in the finish of that race, boring their heads into the wind?"

"I saw them—and their heads twisted out the same

way, when they were putting everything they had into the running."

"D'you think that's chance?" asked Moore.

"It was a queer thing," admitted Silver. "What's the answer?"

"When Mischief got away, long ago, she got away with big Brandy, here, and there's no doubt in my mind—Brandy's the father of Parade."

"Hold on!" exclaimed Silvertip.

"It looks like a long shot, but I think it's a true one. Two horses don't run in a queer way like that, unless there's the same blood in 'em, likely. And look, at the cut of Parade—and then look at Brandy. Years make a difference, but I can remember when Parade and Brandy would've been almost blood brothers at a glance. They got the same cut, but Brandy's finer, and Parade's bigger—and there you are!"

"You'll be telling me," said Silvertip, smiling, "that they *know* that they're father and son, and that's why they walk together, like this!"

"There's strange things in this here world," said Charlie Moore, "and that's exactly what I believe."

"All right," answered Silver, good-humoredly. "I'm happy enough to believe anything, today."

"Old son, where might you be bound?" asked Charlie.

"Over yonder!" said Silvertip.

He waved before him toward the shimmer of the desert, alive with the rising of the heat waves, and toward the rugged waves of the mountains, that gave back on either side from a pass.

"Over the pass?" said Charlie Moore.

"Yes, over the edge of the world, somewhere," said Silvertip. "I've spent a life, so far, trying to find one thing that I really wanted. I've got it now, and I'm going to use it. I don't know for what!"

Old Charlie Moore looked on his companion with dreaming eyes for a moment.

"Give a boy a sword, and the man will be a soldier," he murmured. And then he added: "I'd need to be a younger man, and a stronger man, and Brandy a younger horse under me—but if I could follow you, Silver, I know that I'd find what you're goin' to find—the other side of the horizon, and the reason the sky is blue!"